DARK WATER

LANTERN BEACH BLACKOUT, BOOK 1

CHRISTY BARRITT

Copyright © 2020 by Christy Barritt

All rights reserved.

No part of this book may be reproduced in any form or by any electronic or mechanical means, including information storage and retrieval systems, without written permission from the author, except for the use of brief quotations in a book review.

Scripture quotations taken from The Holy Bible, New International Version® NIV®

Copyright © 1973 1978 1984 2011 by Biblica, Inc. TM

Used by permission. All rights reserved worldwide.

COMPLETE BOOK LIST

Squeaky Clean Mysteries:
- #1 Hazardous Duty
- #2 Suspicious Minds
- #2.5 It Came Upon a Midnight Crime (novella)
- #3 Organized Grime
- #4 Dirty Deeds
- #5 The Scum of All Fears
- #6 To Love, Honor and Perish
- #7 Mucky Streak
- #8 Foul Play
- #9 Broom & Gloom
- #10 Dust and Obey
- #11 Thrill Squeaker
- #11.5 Swept Away (novella)
- #12 Cunning Attractions
- #13 Cold Case: Clean Getaway

#14 Cold Case: Clean Sweep
#15 Cold Case: Clean Break
#16 Cleans to an End (coming soon)
While You Were Sweeping, A Riley Thomas Spinoff

The Sierra Files:
#1 Pounced
#2 Hunted
#3 Pranced
#4 Rattled

The Gabby St. Claire Diaries (a Tween Mystery series):
The Curtain Call Caper
The Disappearing Dog Dilemma
The Bungled Bike Burglaries

The Worst Detective Ever
#1 Ready to Fumble
#2 Reign of Error
#3 Safety in Blunders
#4 Join the Flub
#5 Blooper Freak
#6 Flaw Abiding Citizen
#7 Gaffe Out Loud
#8 Joke and Dagger
#9 Wreck the Halls

#10 Glitch and Famous (coming soon)

Raven Remington
Relentless 1
Relentless 2 (coming soon)

Holly Anna Paladin Mysteries:
#1 Random Acts of Murder
#2 Random Acts of Deceit
#2.5 Random Acts of Scrooge
#3 Random Acts of Malice
#4 Random Acts of Greed
#5 Random Acts of Fraud
#6 Random Acts of Outrage
#7 Random Acts of Iniquity

Lantern Beach Mysteries
#1 Hidden Currents
#2 Flood Watch
#3 Storm Surge
#4 Dangerous Waters
#5 Perilous Riptide
#6 Deadly Undertow

Lantern Beach Romantic Suspense
Tides of Deception
Shadow of Intrigue
Storm of Doubt

Winds of Danger
Rains of Remorse

Lantern Beach P.D.
On the Lookout
Attempt to Locate
First Degree Murder
Dead on Arrival
Plan of Action

Lantern Beach Escape
Afterglow (a novelette)

Lantern Beach Blackout
Dark Water
Safe Harbor
Ripple Effect

Carolina Moon Series
Home Before Dark
Gone By Dark
Wait Until Dark
Light the Dark
Taken By Dark

Suburban Sleuth Mysteries:
Death of the Couch Potato's Wife

Fog Lake Suspense:
- Edge of Peril
- Margin of Error
- Brink of Danger
- Line of Duty

Cape Thomas Series:
- Dubiosity
- Disillusioned
- Distorted

Standalone Romantic Mystery:
- The Good Girl

Suspense:
- Imperfect
- The Wrecking

Sweet Christmas Novella:
- Home to Chestnut Grove

Standalone Romantic-Suspense:
- Keeping Guard
- The Last Target
- Race Against Time
- Ricochet
- Key Witness
- Lifeline

High-Stakes Holiday Reunion

Desperate Measures

Hidden Agenda

Mountain Hideaway

Dark Harbor

Shadow of Suspicion

The Baby Assignment

The Cradle Conspiracy

Trained to Defend

Nonfiction:

Characters in the Kitchen

Changed: True Stories of Finding God through Christian Music (out of print)

The Novel in Me: The Beginner's Guide to Writing and Publishing a Novel (out of print)

CHAPTER ONE

ELISE OLIVER JOLTED upright in her bed, imaginary critters scrambling over her skin. What was that sound? Was someone inside her house?

As her heart thumped in her ears, silence stretched around her. She was certain she'd heard something. The noise had jostled her from her slumber and electrified her senses.

She waited. Breathed in and out. In and out. In and out. For the past week, she'd feared this very moment. Yet, shock still coursed through her.

Dear Lord, give me strength right now.

She reached into her dresser and grabbed her gun. She checked the magazine. The bullets lined up like an army.

Elise thought that would comfort her more, but it didn't.

What would Daniel tell her right now? Elise knew. He'd tell her she couldn't sit here helplessly and wait for this to play out on someone else's terms. Being proactive could save her life.

That was when she heard it again. Somewhere from within the depths of her house, a creak whispered warning of approaching danger.

Someone was here, and Elise knew exactly what they were coming for.

She lowered her legs to the floor and rushed to the corner behind her bedroom door.

Just in time. The creaks moved closer. The intruder was almost to her second-story room.

She gripped her gun and crouched behind the door. This wasn't the best hiding place, but finding another spot was off the table. This would have to work.

Elise squeezed her eyes shut. How was this nightmare even real?

But she already knew that answer also. She just wasn't ready to accept it.

The floor moaned outside her door. The wooden boards in this old house had always been like a blabbermouthed friend. Right now, however, Elise was thankful for their spilled secrets.

Elise's lungs tightened as she saw the shadow under her doorway. This was it, the make-or-break moment. The instant where she would either prevail or where the bad guy would win.

For Daniel's sake, Elise couldn't let the bad guy win. She had to fight with everything in her.

The silver handle turned, and, in slow motion, the door opened.

Elise's gaze shot to her bed. She must have instinctively pulled the blankets back across the mattress. In the dark, it almost appeared she still lay there.

Good. That would buy her some time.

She grasped the gun tighter, praying that she wouldn't have to use it. She'd never pulled the trigger on an actual person before, only on a target at the shooting range. She'd dedicated her entire life to helping people heal. She hated the thought of causing someone harm instead.

But this intruder, though he was faceless, was not a good person. He was dangerous. Deadly. He needed to be stopped.

A man dressed in black slipped into her room.

Elise knew the man could overpower her. She had a gun. So did he, probably. Not only that, but this intruder was most likely better at using his weapon and wouldn't hesitate to pull the trigger . . . whereas Elise would. That put her at a disadvantage.

Sweat trickled down her forehead and back. Elise wished she could disappear. That she somehow wouldn't be found in her hiding spot. But wishful thinking would get her nowhere.

The man stepped closer to the bed. Something about the way he moved made Elise think he was a professional. This was a man who knew what he was doing, who knew how to be stealthy, sneaky.

That made him even more dangerous.

He paced to her bed and reached forward.

He was about to find out Elise wasn't there.

Elise held her breath.

She had to make her move.

Now.

She skulked from around the door, careful not to hit the creaky spots on the floor. Slowly, carefully, Elise slipped into the hallway. She gave one last glance over her shoulder.

The man in black hadn't looked back yet.

Still gripping the gun, Elise tiptoed forward. She just needed to make it to the stairs. If she could get out the front door, she could run to her car.

She could do this. She *had* to do this. Ever since Daniel had died, she'd felt like she was in a daze. But the past week had reignited something in her. She now had a mission. A reason to continue forward.

She slipped farther down the hallway. She still didn't hear the man behind her. Certainly, he'd realized she wasn't in bed now and would begin searching.

Her foot hit the stair. As it did, Elise looked back.

The black shadow appeared in the doorway.

She swallowed a scream as a jolt of panic rushed through her.

Run!

She scrambled down the steps, desperation fueling her actions.

Behind her, the man grunted as he sprinted after her.

Elise reached the first floor. Only a few feet, and she'd be at the front door. If she could just run outside . . .

As she lunged for the handle, the man tackled her. Her head hit the wood floor, and the gun skittered from her grasp.

"Where is it?" The man straddled her, his weight pressing on her lungs.

Elise glanced across the floor and saw her gun lying a few feet away. Just out of reach. What was she going to do?

Think, Elise. Think.

The man leaned down until she felt his moist, rancid breath on her cheek. "Where . . . is . . . it?"

"I don't know what you're talking about." Elise forced the words out through gritted teeth.

He would know that was a lie. Elise knew it was a lie, but she needed to buy herself more time.

"You're going to give it to me. Now." He grabbed her hair and yanked it until Elise yelped.

"Get off me." Elise tried to thrash but couldn't. He'd rendered her immobile.

"You're not the one calling the shots here." His low voice seemed to slither from his lips as his scorching breath flooded over her ear and face. Elise held back her tears as she felt her hair being ripped from her scalp.

She yelped again.

This man enjoyed seeing people suffer. It went against everything Elise believed in. The reality of what he might do sent a shockwave through her system.

She had to think of a way out of this. Unless she gave him that information, this was only the beginning of her pain.

"Okay." Elise gasped, her scalp burning. "I'll give it to you."

He loosened his grip on her hair. Silence stretched, as if he contemplated his next step. Finally, he shifted, and the pressure on her chest eased.

Elise sucked in a deep breath, grateful for relief.

The next instant, the man jerked her to her feet. His strong grasp dug into her arm until she cried out in pain, and a metallic taste flooded her mouth. She must have bitten her cheek.

She dared to look at the man again. All she saw was his massive size. The rest of his features were concealed.

"Where is it?" The man bared his teeth like a dog threatening to fight to the death.

Elise had to think quickly. To think about survival. "It's in the kitchen."

"I looked there."

This must be the guy who'd ransacked her house two days ago.

"I hid it somewhere people wouldn't find it." Elise's voice trembled as she said the words, as she questioned her choice. He'd kill her when he discovered the truth. Her mind raced.

"I looked *everywhere*."

"Not everywhere. My husband taught me a few things."

"Show me." The man dragged Elise into the kitchen, her feet unable to keep up as she stumbled forward.

Her muscles quivered under the weight of what she was about to do. If Elise gave this information to the man, the intel would be destroyed. The bad guys would never be brought to justice. Her husband would continue to look like a traitor.

Elise couldn't let that happen. Too much was on the line.

"It's in there." She pointed to the cabinet beneath the sink. "There's a false bottom."

"Show me." He released her arm and shoved her forward.

Swallowing hard, Elise bent down and opened the door. It squeaked in protest. The sound caused a chill to wash through her.

Elise posed her hand as if she were going to pull the wood from the bottom. Instead, she grabbed a spray bottle of cleaner. She swung around and squeezed the lever.

Bleach hit the man's eyes.

He grabbed his face, muttering obscenities beneath his breath.

His grip loosened. Elise lunged away, desperately clawing the floor as she tried to escape.

It worked. Her attacker still held his face, still yelled with pain.

Rising to her feet, Elise darted toward the door. She grabbed her purse, thankful it had been left on a table near the entry, before stumbling outside.

Her head swam, but she couldn't slow down. If she did, she wouldn't live to see the light of morning.

Only one person could help her.

Colton Locke.

She had to find him if she wanted to survive.

COLTON LOCKE BRISTLED as he observed the crowd in front of him. The sight reminded him of waves lapping the shore. Almost as if one entity, they pushed forward before inching back over and over again. This had been going on for the past forty minutes.

This was American democracy at work. The right to free speech. These were the very freedoms Colton and his men had fought for—that they'd put their lives on the line for.

As he stood guard, a man lunged toward the yellow line that had been strung around the property. "You can't stop me!"

Colton shifted to the left. The man rammed into Colton's chest before bouncing back. Colton didn't budge.

The man slowly drew his dazed eyes up. All it took was one look from Colton, and the protester stepped back. The man opened his mouth, as if tempted to apologize for touching Colton.

Colton had been told he had that effect on people.

"You're on their side?" the man muttered.

"I'm on no one's side," Colton said. "I'm just here to do a job."

"I doubt that." The man shook his head and backed away. "You're going to regret this."

Colton doubted that. People's emotions about the sale of this land were frantic and passionate—almost to an extreme.

"You doing okay over here?" Police Chief Cassidy Chambers paced over to him, one hand on her radio and the other near her waistband—her gun—as if prepared for trouble.

Nearly one hundred people had come out to voice their opposition to a new hotel that had been proposed on this property at Lantern Beach. The land had been foreclosed on, and now a bank in Raleigh owned it. All they cared about was selling it to the highest bidder. All the residents here today cared about was preserving their way of life.

Colton couldn't fault them for that. But laws still needed to be obeyed.

"I'm doing fine." Colton didn't take his eyes off the crowd in front of him. "For a small town, the people certainly have a lot of passion."

"You can say that again." Cassidy's words sounded dry, maybe even exhausted.

Two feet away, another protester tried to dart past the line they'd strung around the area.

Colton reached over and grabbed the man by his shirt. "Where do you think you're going?"

"I'm going to stop those guys." The man pointed to the land in the distance.

"There's no one here yet." Colton kept his voice just above a growl. "There's no one to stop."

The man raised his hands in the air. "Okay, okay. I get it."

Colton glanced at Cassidy and shook his head. Cassidy's expression mirrored his own. She thought this whole thing was both frustrating and slightly amusing. The antics some people used to express their views were persistent, ineffective, and sometimes crazy.

Her radio crackled, and she picked it up. A few minutes later, she pulled out a bullhorn and stood on top of an old stump to address the crowds. "The surveyor is no longer coming today. He was held up on the ferry. You can all go home. Nothing is happening here, and your message has been received."

Moans sounded in the crowd. Everyone here had been prepared to fight for what they believed in.

Cassidy had hired Colton to help with crowd control. He'd been happy to lend a hand. Though Cassidy had three of her officers here, she hadn't been sure how things would shake out. Too many people were upset over this potential development on the island. A surveyor had been scheduled to come today, and the people wanted their voices to be heard.

A few minutes later, the crowd finally began to disperse. No doubt they planned to regroup later. This whole mess was far from over.

"I think we can handle it from here," Cassidy told him. "Thanks for your help."

"No problem."

Colton waited as more people trickled away. Finally, he felt satisfied that he could leave. He sauntered back over to his car, climbed inside, and sat there for a moment.

Life looked a lot different right now than it did a year ago. So much had changed, and Colton was still adjusting. But the ghosts he'd tried to bury deep inside constantly haunted him. Nothing would ever change that.

Nothing.

As he drove back to the cottage where he was staying, he glanced out the window at the sand dunes and the glimpse of ocean beyond them. Even in January, this area was breathtaking.

Lantern Beach, North Carolina, wasn't necessarily the most ideal place to begin an organization like Blackout. The place was secluded and off the beaten path. In fact, the island was only accessible by ferry.

But his friend Ty Chambers had been doing some fantastic work with former military special ops here. It made sense to pull some of those members in to help with an organization like Blackout. The company employed former military to act as security, bodyguards, or to work other high-stakes assignments.

Colton pulled to a stop in front of Ty's place, which served as their temporary headquarters and living area until something more permanent could be established.

A strange car was parked beside the house. Colton slammed his door and looked at the plates.

Virginia.

Who had come here from Virginia? Ty hadn't mentioned anything to Colton about a visitor—not that Ty was obligated to do so. Still, Colton was curious.

Cautiously, he walked up the steps to the screened-in porch that surrounded the front of the house.

When he got to the top, he paused. A woman sat beside the door. Her knees were pulled to her chest, and her eyes appeared dull as she stared off into the distance.

He sucked in a breath as her familiar features came into focus. "Elise?"

Her gaze swerved toward him. "Colton . . . I was hoping you'd be here."

The resounding feeling that something was terribly wrong stretched through him.

Elise Oliver was his best friend's widow.

The woman he hadn't seen in over a year.

How had she ever found him on this secluded island?

It didn't matter. Colton knew with certainty that the only reason she would come here was if she was in trouble.

CHAPTER TWO

SOMETHING SHATTERED inside Colton at the sight of Elise sitting there, looking so broken.

She tried to stand, only to nearly collapse. Colton's arms caught her just in time. She quaked beneath his touch, turning limp.

"I was hoping I'd find you." Her voice cracked as she said the words. "I drove straight here from Virginia Beach."

"Let's get you inside," Colton muttered.

She nodded, but her eyes were glazed. Something was wrong. The thought felt like a punch in the gut.

Colton unlocked the door, took her inside, and lowered her to the couch. "Can I get you something? Some coffee? Water?"

"Coffee would be great. I'm sorry you have to see

me like this. I've been on the road for hours, and I didn't get hardly any sleep."

Colton quickly made a cup for her, his mind racing. Elise. Beautiful Elise, with her dark, chin-length hair. Her pert nose, bright eyes, and smattering of freckles.

Daniel's wife. The woman who haunted his thoughts at night. The woman who made guilt fill him so completely he thought he might drown in the emotion.

Now she was here.

Colton set a steaming mug in front of her and lowered himself beside her on the couch.

In all the years he had known Elise, Colton had never seen her like this. She was always put-together, calm, down-to-earth.

Right now, she wore a sweatshirt and yoga pants. Her eyes look red, as if she'd been crying. And when she shifted, Colton saw the painful gouge on her forehead.

"I'm sorry." Elise ran her sleeve beneath her eyes before meeting his gaze. "But I didn't know where else to go."

"You know you can always come to me if you need anything. Always. What's going on?"

She wiped beneath her eyes again, and her gaze scrambled back-and-forth, as if she struggled to find what to say. Instead, she reached for her coffee.

Her hands trembled so badly she couldn't bring the

mug to her lips. She finally gave up and set it back on the coffee table. She drew in a deep breath, and her gaze met Colton's.

"I'm in trouble," she finally said. "Someone is trying to kill me, and they almost succeeded."

A jolt of concern shot through Colton. Someone trying to kill Elise?

"Is it one of your patients?" It was the only thing that made sense to Colton.

As a psychologist, Elise dealt with people who had severe mental health issues, issues that sometimes affected their judgment. Had one of them decided to take out their grievances on Elise? It was the only explanation Colton could fathom.

He remembered Daniel once telling him about some threats Elise had received from her patients. She'd always brushed them off, called the threats displaced anger. Daniel had said he'd like to displace a few of the people who'd given her so much grief.

Colton understood the notion.

"It's not one of my patients." Elise pulled her legs beneath her, looking more like a little girl than a professional.

Seeing her like this caused something to crack inside him. This was not normal—and that bothered Colton far more than anything else. Whatever happened had obviously rocked Elise's world.

"What's going on, Elise?"

Her wide eyes met his. "I found some information out about Daniel. Now, the wrong person wants it and will do anything to get his hands on it."

ELISE WATCHED as Colton's eyes widened. He looked just as she remembered . . . except something she couldn't quite pinpoint seemed different.

It was his eyes, she thought. They were shadowed, full of much more depth than when they'd first met. Not just depth, though.

Was that anguish? Why? It was too soon to lead with that question.

The man was well over six feet tall, with strapping muscles. His brown hair was a little darker now than it had been when she'd last seen him, and he'd cut it short.

He wasn't the kind of guy people wanted to mess with.

Peeking out from his sleeve, she saw the reminder of the skin graft he'd had after an IED had exploded near him a couple years ago. The injury had almost ended his career, but he'd persevered and joined his SEAL team again.

That fact showed just how strong and determined he was.

Did Colton have any idea what Elise had discovered? Or was he also in the dark about the hidden secrets that waited like a viper ready to strike?

Elise had no clue. But she knew that her husband had always trusted Colton. She knew she could trust the man too.

"Why don't you start from the beginning?" Colton leaned forward, his jaw tight and his brown eyes intense as he waited.

Elise drew in a shaky breath. On the way here, she'd been reviewing everything she knew. She'd been trying to formulate the best way to share the information without coming across sounding paranoid.

She hadn't figured out a good solution. No matter how she tried to frame what she had to say, the facts were going to sound dramatic.

That was because the situation felt more like a Hollywood blockbuster than real life.

She rubbed her trembling hands on her pants and dragged in a deep breath. Her eyes hit the clock in the distance, and she realized the time. Real life flooded back to her.

"I'll tell you everything," she said. "I just need to call into my office first. Let them know I won't be in today. I have patients lined up and—"

"Why don't you use my phone?" Colton pulled it from his pocket. "Tell your staff you're under the weather. Keep it simple."

Elise nodded and took the phone from him. But,

before she could dial, someone else walked into the house. "You're never going to believe this."

Elise turned and saw Griff McIntyre standing in the doorway, looking like the bad boy he'd always been. Blond hair a little too long. Toothpick in his mouth. A hardened look in his eyes.

Griff . . . another familiar face. Showing up here was almost like a homecoming for Elise . . . if only circumstances were different.

He stared at his phone, not even looking to see who was in the room. Whatever he saw on the screen obviously consumed him.

"Last night there was a—" Griff froze when he noticed her, and his face lost some of its color. "Elise."

She nodded, her head clearing just a little. "Hi, Griff."

"I thought you were . . ." He looked at his phone and frowned.

Elise sensed something wasn't as it seemed. "You thought I was what?"

His frown deepened. "I thought you were dead."

CHAPTER THREE

I THOUGHT YOU WERE DEAD. What in the world was Griff talking about?

Colton stared at his friend, anxious to hear his explanation. "Why would you think that, Griff?"

Griff swallowed hard and held up his phone. "I was coming in here to tell you about an article I just read. I have alerts set up on my account. Whenever there's a new article connected with someone from our platoon —or a spouse—I get a notification."

Colton suspected there was more to Griff's curiosity than that, but he said nothing. Griff had probably set that alert in order to see who the next team member might be who was framed.

Nausea rolled in Colton's stomach at the thought.

"I got an alert just now," Griff continued. "It's all over the news that your house caught fire last night,

Elise. Officials believe a gas line exploded. A body was discovered inside."

Elise pinched the skin between her eyes. "No . . ."

Colton's hand came down on her shoulder. "Was anyone in your house when you left?"

"Just the man who attacked me. Who . . . ? How . . . ? I don't understand."

Attacked her? Colton's stomach tightened as a protectiveness rose in him. He would find whoever had done this. No one would stop him.

He softened his voice before saying, "We'll get to the bottom of this. Let's just take this step by step."

Elise nodded, but she still held her head, as if overwhelmed by the news she'd just heard.

"Anything else, Griff?"

"No, they haven't released any more details yet."

"If you hear anymore, let me know."

"Of course." Griff nodded. "I'll give you guys some time. Elise . . . it's good to see you."

"Thanks, Griff. You too." But Elise sounded less than convincing. Her gaze turned back to Colton. "The past week has been like a nightmare."

"I want to hear about it. But, Elise, I wouldn't call your office. Not yet. Maybe the best thing right now is for people to think you're dead."

"But . . ."

"It's your choice. But if you can disappear for a while, then I think you should."

ELISE SUCKED in a deep breath before diving in. This felt like one of her husband's underwater missions. The stakes were just as high, just as intense. But she felt ill-equipped for the role.

She glanced at Colton, at his penetrating gaze as he waited for her to gather her thoughts. Daniel had always called him a rock—dependable, solid, the kind of person everyone should have in their lives.

"I found evidence to prove Daniel may not have been a traitor after all," she finally said. The words felt surreal as they left her lips.

Colton's breath caught beside her. He'd never believed Daniel was guilty. Neither did Elise. It didn't matter what everybody else thought, Colton and Elise knew Daniel better than anyone. They knew he was honorable.

"What did you find?" Colton's voice sounded deep, throaty.

"A couple things, including a burner phone. I charged it and saw several calls made to the same number within the US. I couldn't trace the number, however. I also found what appears to be a coded message and several photos." Her gaze remained on Colton as she waited for his reaction.

"What did you do after you found those things?"

"I went to the command office. It seemed like the

logical thing to do, and I thought the team there would want to know what I had discovered. I met with both Commander Larson and Secretary Stabler—"

"Secretary of the Navy Stabler?" Colton asked, surprise lilting his voice.

"That's right. He just happened to be there when I arrived. I told them what I'd discovered, and they promised to look into it."

"What happened next?" Colton asked. "Did they seem concerned?"

"Not really." She shrugged. "I mean, they kept giving each other looks. I'm pretty sure Secretary Stabler couldn't care less about Daniel at this point. He only thinks of him as a traitor. The whole meeting probably only lasted ten minutes, and then I was back at my car and sent on my merry way."

"How did that lead to you coming here?" Colton continued to push.

"After the meeting, I began to feel that somebody was watching me. Following me. My house was broken into, but nothing was stolen." She drew in a shaky breath. "Then last night someone came into my house with a gun and demanded that I give him the information."

Colton bristled. "Did he hurt you?"

Elise touched her forehead, feeling her eyes cloud as she remembered the stark fear she'd felt during those moments. She was lucky to be alive right now. "He banged me up pretty well, but I'm okay."

Colton gently ran his finger beneath the cut on her forehead. "You should be checked out by a doctor, just to be safe."

"No, I'll be fine. Really. I have other things to worry about right now." Images from last night hit her again, each one causing her to flinch. "I got away and started running. I knew I needed help, that this was bigger than me. So I managed to track down where you were, and I came straight here. I didn't know what else to do."

"You did the right thing." Colton's voice was unwavering, as was his gaze. "We'll help you."

"Thank you." Her voice quivered. She knew that Colton would help. He was that kind of guy, cut from the same cloth as Daniel had been. She was thankful she had someone to turn to.

"Come to the bathroom. I need to clean that cut."

She didn't argue. She followed Colton through the house. In the bathroom, she sat on the counter as Colton directed. He found a first aid kit and brushed her hair off her forehead to examine the cut.

"Nothing a couple of butterfly bandages can't fix," he murmured.

She said nothing, just waited as he pulled out some antiseptic cream and blotted her wound.

"Where is this information you found?" Colton

used some gauze to wipe away the excess ointment. "Did you hand it over to someone?"

"No, I hid it."

A grin of approval spread across Colton's face. "Good girl. We're going to probably need to see that."

"I figured you might. I figured *somebody* might."

"The commander didn't ask you for it?"

"I told him I'd put it somewhere safe and didn't feel right carrying it with me."

"Did he offer to send someone to get it?" Colton pulled off the back of a bandage.

Something about his closeness made it hard for Elise to breathe. Probably the fact that he'd been her husband's best friend. They shouldn't be this close. But the act was innocent. Colton was just treating her cut. Her reaction didn't make sense.

She cleared her throat. "They did. I told them I was more comfortable keeping it until I knew the next step. They brushed me off. Based on their reaction, I didn't think they were all that interested in it. Or maybe I figured they didn't take me seriously. I'm not sure. The whole meeting was strange."

Colton carefully pressed the bandage to her forehead and then stepped back. "Did you bring it with you today?"

"I brought a copy."

Elise knew she needed to hand it over. But, by doing so, she felt like she was opening Pandora's box.

Elise only hoped she didn't bring destruction on all of them.

Just as the thought entered her mind, an explosion rocked the house.

Had the man from last night already found her?

CHAPTER FOUR

COLTON GRABBED Elise's arms to steady her.

What was that? The whole cottage had quaked. Pictures rattled. The soap dish vibrated.

"Stay here." Moving quickly, Colton darted into the living room. He glanced around. Everything appeared to be intact. But he didn't relax yet.

Instead, he ran out onto the screened-in porch and scanned the area. He sucked in a breath at what he saw.

Elise's car.

A ball of fire surrounded it.

There was only one thing that could have caused an explosion like that.

A bomb.

Someone had left a bomb in Elise's car. Colton felt

certain of it. She was fortunate that she hadn't been inside when it went off.

Had the device been on a timer? Or had someone chosen this moment to detonate it? Either way, he didn't like this.

"Colton?"

He looked over and saw Elise standing at the door, a knot between her fear-filled eyes.

"It's going to be okay," he said.

She stepped outside and stood beside him, staring at the carnage of her vehicle. Colton slipped an arm around her, and she seemed to sag against him.

"Was I . . . was I supposed to be inside?" she muttered.

"I don't know." Colton pulled out his phone. "We need to get someone out here, though. They're probably already on their way. I'm sure everyone within a quarter mile heard that."

Elise still stared at her vehicle. The initial blast had died down, but flames still shot from every part of the car.

"That could have been me . . ." she muttered.

"Let's just be thankful it wasn't."

She nodded but looked unconvinced. Looked in shock, for that matter.

Whatever was going on, it was serious. Dead serious.

THE POLICE CAME five minutes later, along with the fire department. The flames around Elise's car were extinguished. Investigators were examining the vehicle and the police had taken a report. Colton and Elise had been dismissed to go back inside for now.

After the bomb—or what remained of it—was retrieved from the carnage, maybe they'd have more answers. Colton was thankful no one had been hurt and that the car was far enough from the house that there was no further damage.

As Colton led Elise back inside, memories hit him. Memories that he'd tried desperately to forget. Memories of the battlefield, and the battlefield was what he'd come here to get away from.

That last black ops mission he'd worked had nearly destroyed him. It had nearly destroyed them *all*. In fact, Blackout had formed as a direct result of that day. This subsection of Colton's platoon had needed a break from the military after things had gone terribly wrong.

Daniel was dead, and Elise was a widow trying to navigate life by herself.

Not only that, but now she apparently needed to navigate danger as well.

Guilt pounded at him. If Colton had been more on

top of things that day, Daniel might still be alive. Elise might not be a widow.

Even worse, she still didn't know the whole story about how her husband had died.

More guilt nipped at Colton.

Elise had already been through so much. She didn't need this on top of everything else. But whatever she'd found must have made someone feel threatened.

Was the person who'd attacked her the same person who'd sold them out before their last operation? His higher-ups had believed that person was Daniel, but Colton knew that wasn't the case.

To the day Colton died, he would never believe that Daniel had done the things he was accused of doing. Daniel was the type of guy Colton trusted with his life, not the kind who would have sold his soul to fatten his wallet.

As they lowered themselves at the table, Elise looked like she was beside herself. If her trembling hands were a reflection of her inner turmoil then she was a mess. He poured her a fresh cup of coffee before sitting down beside her.

Colton couldn't stand watching Elise like this. He reached for her hands. Two of her hands easily fit within one of his. He pressed them together, trying to calm her trembles.

"Just take a deep breath," he coached. "When

you're ready, tell me, where did you find this information?"

Slowly, Elise breathed in, then out, before nodding and beginning. "In Daniel's office."

"He had an office at your house?"

"That's right." She looked out the window, her gaze hooded. "He spent a lot of time there. I'm sure you know that the past two years of our marriage were hard. Daniel and I talked about separating. We might as well have been separated as much as we saw each other."

Colton bit down. Daniel had alluded to those facts, but Colton hadn't wanted to bring them up. Instead, he nodded, trying to remain neutral. Their marriage wasn't his business.

"You know what the statistics are," Elise continued. "Ninety percent of marriages within the Navy SEAL community fail. I was determined that Daniel and I weren't going to be one of those statistics. But he hadn't been acting like himself. When he was home, he was distant, like something bothered him. Something he wouldn't acknowledge."

Colton knew what Elise was talking about. He'd seen the shift in Daniel also. Some people assumed those changes indicated he was guilty, that he was involved in things he shouldn't be. But Colton knew the speculation wasn't true.

Based on what Elise had just told him and what he'd just seen . . . the mystery surrounding Daniel and his death was far from over.

And now Elise was caught in the crossfire in a battle she'd never signed up to fight.

CHAPTER FIVE

COLTON WAITED for Elise to continue.

"When he returned home from this last deployment, we were going to really try to fix the broken parts of our relationship. But we never had that chance." Elise looked down at her hands—the ones Colton still gripped—as her voice trailed off with grief.

Colton gave her a moment to compose herself, even as his heart twisted inside his chest.

"Anyway," Elise started again, "I decided that I needed to do something different with his office. Honestly, I wanted to forget the fact that we'd even had our problems. The place had almost become like a war room to him. Daniel was in there all the time, wanting to be by himself, working on things he couldn't tell me about. I know the office wasn't the cause of our problems, but I've always associated the two together."

"And?" Colton waited for her to continue.

"I decided I would replace the flooring. He'd always hated that floor anyway—it was ugly tan carpet. I decided to remove it myself."

Colton felt the start of a smile at the corner of his lips. Elise had always been a go-getter. Once she got an idea in her head, she didn't let it go.

That was probably the reason why her marriage to Daniel had lasted as long as it had. It was also the reason why she was able to get her doctorate in psychology while her husband had been serving overseas. She was one determined woman, and Colton had always admired her for that.

"As I was pulling up the carpet, I noticed a section of the subfloor had been cut out. I knew that the carpet in that area was a little loose, but I didn't think much of it. Out of curiosity, I pried the wood up, and I was surprised to see a metal box stashed beneath the floor. I found all the information there." Her gaze swerved up to meet Colton's. "I thought the only people who hid things like these were CIA operatives. That's the way it happens in the movies, at least."

"When you work with the people we work with, sometimes there's a lot more CIA in us than we would like to admit," Colton said. "Clandestine information is something you have to be careful with."

"Either way, I found it. I assume Daniel thought he would come home and use this information himself. Or maybe he hid it away hoping I might find it one day if things went south. I don't really know. Maybe you do, and maybe one day, if you're comfortable enough, you can share that information with me."

Colton didn't say anything. The more information Elise knew, the more danger she would be in. He didn't want to put her in that position.

He released her hands. They'd stopped trembling. She leaned forward and picked up her coffee mug, this time successfully bringing it to her lips without spilling it. She took a long drink before setting it down again.

"Everything I found has been documented on this SD card." She reached into her purse and pulled it out. "I'm hoping that you can make sense of it. I took pictures of everything."

"Pictures?"

"I bought a digital camera and decided this was the best way to ensure I got the information to the right people. I hid the originals."

"Let's see what you've got," Colton said.

But he already didn't like the sound of this. Not at all.

ELISE FELT her hands begin to sweat. After what had

happened at her house and to her car, could she really blame herself?

Colton grabbed a computer from the table and slid the SD card into the slot. They both stared at the screen as lines and lines of various numbers appeared.

Colton squinted at the images. "What are these?"

"I tried to figure it out," Elise said. "But I didn't get very far. I hope I didn't sit on this for too long. I was trying to figure out how to handle this the best way."

"I'm glad you came here. You did the right thing."

Just hearing Colton's affirmation brought her a wave of comfort. Elise was so thankful now that she had been able to find him.

It hadn't been easy, especially since she didn't want to alert anyone as to her whereabouts. But Elise had used the burner phone she bought after fleeing her house to do some research. Eventually, she'd found a small article that mentioned Colton being in Lantern Beach.

Even better was the fact that there were other former Navy SEALs here with him. Maybe, between all of them, they would have some insight as to how to handle this.

Colton turned toward her. "Okay, let's think this through. I know we're only skimming the surface here. But you found information that seems to implicate someone. The fact that Daniel was hiding it indicates this was most likely high-level. The fact that he didn't share it with anyone else, including any of the guys on his team, also meant that he had good reason to hide it."

Elise was so thankful that Colton hadn't mentioned the theory that Daniel was hiding these things out of guilt. That had been her fear. The worry caused her to lose sleep at night even. Her husband had been a good man. Even with their issues, she'd never doubted that.

"So who could this information be about?" Colton shifted, but his gaze remained on Elise.

"I suppose only Daniel knew that," Elise said. "He never spoke about any of his missions."

Colton's eyes darkened.

The details about exactly what Daniel was doing and where had always been sketchy, and Elise hated being left in the dark. Yet she understood the job and the security clearance necessary. She tried to respect the boundaries, but it was harder than she'd anticipated.

"I just wish things hadn't happened the way they did." Colton's voice turned gravelly and raw. "That . . . that training exercise . . . it will haunt me every day for the rest of my life."

Elise wanted to reach out, to touch his arm, to reassure Colton that she didn't hold him responsible for her husband's death. But when Colton had placed her small hands between his larger ones earlier, something strange happened to her heart. Touching him felt off limits now.

It wasn't that Elise was attracted to Colton, nor was it that she *wasn't* attracted to him. The situation played with her emotions right now. Elise knew better than anybody that feelings were fickle, and she'd be wise to keep that in mind.

"Do you think this information might have something to do with one of your missions?" Elise asked again.

The shadow in Colton's gaze only grew deeper. "It's a definite possibility."

"I know the past few operations seemed to be centered in the same area. Exactly who were the bad guys you were fighting?" The question hung in the air, and she wasn't sure she'd get a response. "Can you tell me that?"

"The Savages." Colton's jaw tightened. "They mostly operate out of northern Africa, in the Mediterranean, and they're the most vicious group I have ever dealt with in all my years being a SEAL."

That wasn't comforting. She knew of the Savages and knew they were brutal. No, more than brutal. They lived up to their name.

They wanted to kill anyone who didn't agree with their views. They were believed to be behind a power outage in New York City a couple years ago, though the media hadn't identified them as the ones responsible.

She'd overheard Daniel saying something about it on the phone once. When Elise had asked him, he told her he couldn't talk about the details and that she should pretend she'd never heard that conversation.

"What else can you tell me about them?" she asked.

"They're pirates who attack boats traveling the route between Africa and the US. They supposedly have ties with more than one corrupt governments in the Middle East region, but there's no proof of that."

"What's their goal?"

"Tantalum. It's used in electronics—cell phones in particular. The substance is also a part of the mineral trade war in the Congo and Rwanda."

"So is this about money?" she asked.

"It's about control. If they control tantalum, they'll control the tech world."

The sinking feeling grew in Elise's gut. "Could the information I found be about one of the Savages? Maybe one of their leaders?"

Colton swallowed hard. "It's a possibility. I've always wondered if the group had somebody on the inside here in the US."

Colton's words echoed through the room, echoed in her head. Certainly Elise hadn't heard correctly. "You think an American citizen is working with them?"

"Yes, that's exactly what I think. I have no proof, only a nagging feeling that I can't shake."

"So if this insider happened to find out that I'd

discovered information that might implicate him or her, that would be a really good reason to come after me, wouldn't you say?" Elise thought having answers would comfort her—it didn't.

Colton's gaze locked with hers. "Yes, I'd say that would be a very good reason. However, you said the only people you mentioned this to were at the command center, correct?"

"That's correct."

He leaned back and rubbed his jaw. "The information could have somehow been relayed another way."

Elise's back straightened. "What do you mean?

"Before you went to the command, did you call anybody or talk to anybody in your home about it?"

"Only the commander. Why? What are you getting at?"

"I'm wondering if somehow your house or your phone was bugged."

Elise felt the color leave her face at the thought of it. "You think somebody would've gone that far?"

"I *know* somebody would've gone that far, especially if they thought Daniel had secrets. Big secrets. Secrets of national security."

She nodded at the pictures on the computer. "Do you think that's what his secret is? Something that could have far-reaching implications?"

"Yes." Not even a smidgen of doubt lingered in Colton's voice.

As the thought tried to settle in her mind, Elise's phone rang. She sucked in a breath as she listened to the ring.

"What?" Colton asked.

"This is a burner phone. I literally just bought it a few hours ago. No one has the number."

"Answer it," Colton said. "Put it on speaker."

With her finger poised on the Talk button, she glanced at Colton. He gave her a subtle nod of affirmation. Elise hit Talk. Before she even said hello, a deep voice came through the line.

"I will get the information one way or another," the caller growled.

Elise's blood went cold. "Who is this?"

"That's not important. Just know this: if I don't get what I want, I'll ruin you."

CHAPTER SIX

COLTON SAW Elise's face go pale. He wanted to reach out to comfort her, but he stopped himself. Elise was a strong, professional woman who didn't need to be coddled. He knew that.

But there was part of Elise that had always captured his heart. She was everything he'd ever wanted in a significant other . . . but she'd been married to his best friend. She had been—and always would be—off limits.

I will get the information one way or another. Just know this: if I don't get what I want, I'll ruin you.

The phone call had abruptly ended after that last line.

Whoever was behind this was sick—and there was a good chance he was connected to the mission where Daniel had died. Colton had suspected for a while that there was more to that operation than met the eye, but every lead he'd investigated turned up nothing.

"How did someone get this number?" Elise's face looked at least three shades lighter.

That was a great question. "You said you got the phone a few hours ago?"

"That's right. On the way here. I only activated it on the ferry."

The sinking feeling in Colton's gut only grew deeper. "If someone was following you, they could have seen you purchase it. Could have gotten the code from the clerk at the store and then traced it."

She pressed her eyes closed. "And I thought I was being so smart."

"It was a smart move. You probably slowed him down. No doubt someone could have been monitoring your regular cell—following you, even listening in on your calls. You were wise to leave it behind."

"That doesn't make me feel better." Elise folded her hands in her lap, looking demure despite the storm raging in her gaze. "I keep thinking about my car exploding."

"I have a feeling a device was planted there as a backup plan, in case you managed to get away."

"Did this guy mean to kill me?"

"Maybe the person behind this set off the bomb to let you know there's nowhere you'll be out of reach.

You did the right thing by coming here. We can keep you safe."

"Will they find me here?" She swallowed hard.

Colton bit down, his thoughts hovering between the blunt truth or the sugarcoated version. He decided to be forthcoming. "They probably already know you're here."

Elise sucked in a quick breath. "Really? You think so? Then maybe I should go somewhere—"

"They'll find you wherever you go," he said. "There's a chance they also left a tracking device on your car with the bomb. But, if that didn't work, they'd find another way."

Elise remained quiet a beat, as if processing his words. Then she startled back to the present. "I don't know what to say."

"I don't know for certain who this guy is, but I know he's dangerous. Whether he's working with the Savages or another terrorist organization, he has no respect for human life. And he's smart. Daniel wouldn't have gathered the information otherwise. He wouldn't have kept it a secret."

Unless it implicated him. Colton kept that thought to himself. He'd never for a moment wondered if Daniel was guilty of the things he'd been accused of. He knew his friend better than that. But that's what his accusers would say. It was probably what Commander Larson and Secretary Stabler thought and why they'd brushed Elise off.

"I'm on borrowed time, aren't I?" Elise's wide eyes seemed to beg him for reassurance.

"You're in the safest place that you can be right now. I have the most highly qualified, highly trained men in the world right here. Now we just need to figure out how to find answers so you don't have to live like this for the rest of your life."

She nodded but said nothing.

"Listen, let me call Ty—Ty Chambers. You remember him?"

She nodded again.

"I'm sure he'd be more than happy to let you stay here."

"I don't want to be an inconvenience."

"You won't be. You're family." Colton picked up his phone. "Did you bring anything with you?"

"Just my purse."

It looked like Colton's plans had changed for this week. There weren't many people that Colton would put his life on hold for.

But Elise was one of them.

CHAPTER SEVEN

AN HOUR LATER, Elise stood in her room wearing clean clothes and with freshly washed hair. Her scalp was still achy from where the man had torn out her hair. But she'd managed to wash and style it somewhat.

She paused in front of the dresser mirror and frowned at her reflection. The vibrant person she'd once been seemed to be fading, replaced by this woman with dull eyes and a lackluster expression. What if it wasn't possible to recover from this situation?

The whole situation felt overwhelming. Bigger than what she was capable of.

At least she had Colton to help her.

She sighed and closed her eyes.

Elise needed to gather her thoughts, but her mind was all over the place.

Whose body could that have been inside her house? Why had someone burned it down? Had someone really planted a bomb in her car?

It had obviously been put there to send a message. If she was dead, the person behind this couldn't get the information he so desired.

Nothing made sense.

But the danger that pressed on her made it hard to take a breath. What would this person try next?

Pushing aside those thoughts, Elise ventured from her room. She followed the scent of something savory down the hall and back to the kitchen. She sucked in a breath at what she saw there.

Daniel's crew.

Griff McIntyre. He was the silent, brooding one of the group. But there'd always been a turbulence in his eyes.

Dez Rodriquez. The man's dad was Cuban, his mom was American, and Dez himself was 100 percent charisma and confidence.

And Colton, of course.

Elise hadn't seen the team since Daniel's memorial service. She'd wanted a funeral, but his body had never been found. She hadn't been able to get the closure she needed.

At the thought of that horrible day, her stomach clenched.

Her husband should have been buried with honor.

Instead, his name had been dragged through the mud and articles had been written about how he'd been a traitor to his country. It wasn't fair.

Then again, no one ever said life was fair. That cliché, however, never made anyone feel better.

As soon as the guys saw her, they all stood from the table and gave her hugs. Elise felt like she was with a group of her brothers right now, and a moment of bittersweet memories washed over her.

There had been so many days when she'd had these guys over for spaghetti dinners. They had all kicked back and relaxed. After devouring a home-cooked meal, they'd watched a game on TV or played cards.

Her and Daniel's home had been a safe place for the team to hang out. Too many SEALs engaged in unsafe behavior when they returned home from deployment, so Daniel had always tried to provide them a healthy outlet. Elise had been totally on board with that. As a psychologist, she knew the effects of high-stakes, adrenaline-charged missions.

A blonde woman in a police uniform stood beside Ty, a warm smile on her face. A golden retriever obediently sat beside them, his tail wagging as he waited for an introduction.

"Elise, it's great to see you." Ty smiled, something almost nostalgic in his voice.

"You too." Ty hadn't been on Daniel's team, but

they'd worked together on occasion. Elise had always liked him.

"I heard you met my wife earlier."

Elise smiled at the police chief. "Yes, we did."

Cassidy extended her hand. "It's nice to officially meet you. Earlier, it was a little hectic, to say the least."

"Yes, it was."

"I'm glad to see the clothes worked out." Cassidy nodded at Elise's outfit.

Elise looked down at the sweatshirt and jeans she wore. "They're perfect. Thank you."

"We'll make sure we get you some clothes that fit real soon."

"This is Kujo." Ty rested his hand on the back of the dog's head.

Elise bent forward and patted the dog on the head. The canine's tail slapped the floor in excitement.

Cassidy pointed to the table. "In the meantime, why don't you have a seat? We are just about to dig into some pot roast. We're having an early dinner tonight."

"Can I help get anything ready?"

"We've got everything covered." Cassidy grabbed a serving spoon from the drawer and slid it into a dish of gravy-covered potatoes and carrots. "But thank you."

Elise found a place at the table beside Colton. Being near him brought a rush of warmth through her. Why did his presence comfort her so much? She'd been doing life alone for the past year, and she hadn't realized the toll it had taken on her.

As the food was served, chitchat passed back and forth among them. Certainly by now Colton had informed the group about what was going on. But Elise appreciated having a break from all the questions. She needed to process everything.

Uncertainty had been hounding her, and Elise wouldn't be escaping it anytime soon. But it was good to see the boys being boys. She and Cassidy exchanged several smiles as they all talked.

"Griff tell you he almost lost that contest with Mayor MacArthur?" Dez said, a sparkle in his eyes. "They tried to see who could scale the side of the mayor's beach house the fastest."

"In my defense, the mayor is lithe. Very lithe. I've got more bulk."

"Keep telling yourself that," Dez said.

A round of chuckles filled the table.

"How was kiteboarding today?" Griff jabbed back at Dez. "I'm sure Delilah was a great teacher."

Dez grinned. "She was. She said I was a natural."

"I'm sure she did." Griff raised his eyebrows. "It's a good thing you do all your manscaping. At least Delilah could appreciate it."

"We're just friends. And there's nothing wrong with a little manscaping." He flexed his muscles, always one to put on a show.

Elise had always found their banter entertaining, and today was no exception. These guys loved to give each other a hard time. When they stopped aggravating each other, that's when she would start to worry.

Colton cleared his throat, as if wanting to change the subject. "How was your day, Cassidy? We're not trying to leave you out."

Cassidy tore a dinner roll in half. "You mean after the circus at the proposed site for the new hotel? And the car bomb? It was pretty uneventful after that."

"Who was that man who threatened me at the protest?" Colton asked. "Did you recognize him?"

"Someone threatened you?" Cassidy raised an eyebrow.

"He was a pretty puny guy. I'm not too worried. But he said I would pay because I'd sided with the developer."

"By defending the property you'd sided with the developer?" Cassidy repeated.

"In this man's mind, yes."

"This must be some pretty important property," Elise said.

"Last year, a cult set up camp here on this island and nearly destroyed us," Cassidy explained, spreading some butter across her roll. "Thankfully, they're gone now, and the leader won't be causing any more problems. The property where their compound was is now up for sale."

"So the fact that someone wants to buy the land is a good thing?" Elise asked, trying to get a feel for the situation.

"The thing is, the people who want to buy it plan to build a hotel. A lot of places might like that, but people around here in Lantern Beach like keeping things simple. People come here because it's like stepping back in time. We don't have any chain restaurants or gas stations or stores. Everything here is locally owned."

"But the other problem is that we have a housing crisis," Ty added. "With so many rentals, it's driven up the price of real estate. Our average, everyday workers can't afford the mortgages, so people are arguing that a solution like this hotel could be a win-win for everybody."

"There's going to be a town meeting tonight," Cassidy said. "It will be interesting to see how things turn out."

"It sounds like it," Elise said. "I hope that goes well."

Cassidy raised her eyebrows. "So do I."

Elise already liked Cassidy. There was something very personable about her. Yet Elise could sense part of her was guarded as well. Elise supposed that, as police chief, Cassidy would need to keep a small circle of those she trusted.

Elise wondered how someone like Cassidy had

ended up here. Something about the woman's mannerisms reminded Elise of someone from the big city. Maybe she would have a chance to ask her later.

Besides, Elise had other bigger issues to worry about at the moment—issues like staying alive.

AFTER THE DISHES were cleaned up from dinner, Colton turned to Elise. He wanted more time to talk with her alone. He also sensed just how difficult this had been for her. Though she tried to smile, Colton saw the pain beneath the action.

"Would you like to go for a walk? It's a pretty mild day out for January, and I thought you might like the chance to stretch your legs. Plus, we might be able to catch the sunset. It's pretty fantastic around here."

"A walk sounds perfect." Elise nodded, as if she'd been looking for something to keep her mind occupied. "So does some fresh air."

A few minutes later, they stepped from the house, crossed the sand dune, and the Atlantic Ocean greeted them. Elise paused there and stared at the vastness for a moment.

Colton watched as she soaked it all in. The wind blew her chin-length hair up in wild currents, but she pulled her sweatshirt closer, seeming undeterred.

"This really is breathtaking." Elise glanced back at

him. "Though I initially wondered why you would've picked such a remote location for your operations, I can see why you and your guys like it here."

Colton crossed his arms and glanced around, keeping his eyes open for trouble. "This goes hand-in-hand with the therapy Ty does with former military members. In fact, if you're ever looking for a job, you should talk to Ty. I'm sure he could use a psychologist."

Elise flashed a quick, distracted smile. "I'll have to keep that in mind."

"You do that."

As they walked closer to the shore, Elise glanced behind her, tension returning to her gaze. "Are you sure it's safe out here?"

Colton could practically see the flashbacks hitting her. Every time he thought about what that man had done to her, red-hot anger burned through his veins. Elise didn't deserve any of this. She was nothing but a kind, good-hearted soul who would never hurt a flea.

"Safe? I can't promise that." Colton had always been one to tell the truth . . . he only wished he could tell Elise how Daniel really died. But confidentiality was something he had to take seriously. National security depended on it.

"Earlier you said the person pursuing me probably knows where I am. So they could see me walking right now."

Colton raised the hem of his shirt just enough to

show the gun tucked into a holster on his belt. "I brought this, just in case. I don't plan on going far."

"Good. Because I don't want to be a prisoner at the house for the entire time I'm here."

"I can respect that."

They paced several steps together, not saying a word. The sand was thick and indulgent, causing their feet to sink with every step. Ty called it sugar sand because it was so soft and pliable. Colton thought the name was fitting.

Finally, Colton gave Elise the update on his plans. "If it's okay with you, I'm going to talk to my guys tonight. I'd like their help on this."

"You're sure we can trust all of them?" Elise asked.

"These are Daniel's guys. If we can't trust them, then who can we trust?" But the words left a bitter taste in his mouth.

Colton wanted to believe he could trust everyone. But flashes of doubt lingered in his mind. To this day, he still believed that someone on the inside had leaked information to the Savages. That was the only explanation as to why their mission had torpedoed out of control, the only reason to explain Daniel's death.

Elise nodded slowly, somberly. "I suppose you're correct. I'm not trying to question you. I'm just on edge about all of this."

"Anyone in your shoes would be." Colton paused,

and his tone softened as he glanced at her. Her perky features, intelligent eyes, and petite build were a sight to see. "You look good, Elise."

Surprise filled her gaze before her lips pulled up in a half-smile. "Thanks. You don't look too shabby yourself. How long have you been here in Lantern Beach?"

"I came last May to help Ty out with Hope House. While I was here, I had the crazy idea to start Blackout. We spent several months trying to get the details right and file the proper paperwork. We officially started a few months ago."

"It sounds like a great idea. I'm glad to see you guys are using your gifts."

"It feels like this is what we were made to do, you know?" Colton said.

"I think that's fantastic. People who have purpose are happier and more satisfied with their lives. It might sound like psychobabble, but it's true."

They walked a few more steps, and Elise shivered. As the sun began to set, the temperature grew more frigid. Colton took off the jacket he wore and draped it over her shoulders.

The grateful smile that Elise offered him was enough thanks. "You don't have to do this. You're going to get cold."

"I don't mind. And thank you for trusting me with this information." The words left Colton's lips, sincerity etched in each of them. It meant a lot to him to know Elise had turned to him for help.

"I knew right away you were the only one who could help." Elise offered another smile.

Colton had so much he wanted to ask her. He wanted to know about her life over the past year. He wanted to know if she'd been able to pick up the pieces yet. If she'd moved on. If she'd started seeing anyone else.

But Colton didn't feel it was his place to bring those things up. Not yet, at least.

"I've always hated the water," Elise said as she stared at the ocean. "Don't get me wrong, I love looking at it. Dipping my feet in. But being in over my head? I hate it. I'm a psychologist. I know what that means. I feel like I lose control when I'm out deep."

"Yet you married a SEAL."

"Yes, I did. I would have never gotten through BUD/S, not even the first day." BUD/S was the underwater portion of SEAL training. It was where the majority of candidates realized they weren't going to make the cut.

Colton smiled.

"I'm in deep right now, Colton." Her voice trembled.

He stepped closer and lowered his voice. "I'm here to make sure you don't drown."

Movement in the distance caught his eye. He stiffened as a figure lumbered over the dune less than a block away.

The man's gaze went straight to Elise, and he started toward her.

Colton grabbed his gun and prepared himself to react.

CHAPTER EIGHT

ELISE SAW the man charging toward them and froze. In the blink of an eye, Colton nudged himself in front of her and drew his gun.

At once, the implications of the situation hit her. Had this man followed her here? Would he finish what had been started back at her house? Elise flinched as she remembered the fear she'd felt as she waited for that man to catch her. She remembered the pain of being thrown to the floor. The pure desperation to get away.

Her head swam. She'd been a fool to think she could run from it. Colton was right—trouble had followed her here.

"Stay back!" Colton shouted.

The man stopped and put his hands in the air. "Didn't mean any problems."

Colton didn't seem to buy it. His muscles remained tight. "Who are you, and what are you doing here?"

"I live here. On the beach."

As the man said the words, Elise got a better look at his features. The man wore multiple layers, and his skin looked dirty and unwashed, as did his hair.

Was he homeless?

"You don't need to be hanging out on this part of the beach." Colton's voice still sounded as hard as steel.

"Okay, okay, man." The guy took a step back, his hands still in the air. "Not trying to cause any trouble. Just looking for a place to settle down and enjoy the day."

"Find it on another part of the beach." Colton reached into his pocket and pulled out some bills. With gun still in hand, he extended his other arm toward the man. "Take this. Get yourself something to eat or a room at the inn for the night."

The man nodded quickly and shoved the money into his pocket. "Thanks. I won't bother you again. Sorry."

Colton waited until the man disappeared over the sand dune before putting the gun back into his holster. When he turned to face Elise, she felt her bones turning into JELL-O.

How much more of this could she take? Would she be jumping at every stranger she saw until this was resolved? And, for that matter, would this ever truly be resolved?

She was unsure about what the future held, and that left her feeling uneasy.

She pulled her gaze up to meet Colton's and saw him studying her. He was worried. She had no doubt about that.

"Thank you," she finally croaked out, rubbing her throat with one hand and pulling Colton's jacket tighter around her with the other. The soothing scent of leather filled her senses, bringing her a moment of comfort.

"Thankfully, it was a false alarm. But we do need to be on guard."

She nodded, probably too rapidly. Usually, she worked hard to remain expressionless, to hide how she really felt. It was part of her job. Her patients couldn't know how horrified she was by some of the things they told her. But, right now, she was having trouble keeping herself in check.

"Yes, I know," she finally said. "Believe me, I know. I feel like I've unleashed something evil, for lack of a better word."

"You didn't do anything, Elise." Colton reached forward and squeezed her bicep. His touch sent a race of heat through her.

A race of heat? Elise had no business feeling anything when Colton touched her. Colton was

Daniel's best friend. Feeling anything for him seemed like such a betrayal.

Besides, she should have done right by Daniel. But she'd failed him. It seemed the ultimate injustice to show grace to one of his friends when she hadn't extended that grace to her own husband.

If only she could go back in time...

She took a step away in an attempt to collect herself. "I should've handled this differently. Stayed quiet. Come straight here. I don't know exactly."

"I would've done the same thing," Colton said.

Surprise rolled through Elise as she looked up into Colton's brown eyes, searching them for a sign of the truth. "Really?"

"Really. The command is supposed to be a safe place."

Something about his response made her lungs freeze, and her tension deepened. "Why do you say, 'supposed to be'?"

He rubbed his jaw like he always did when deep in thought. "Because I've suspected for a while now that someone is covering up something. I don't know who has the answers, and no one is talking. Believe me, I've tried to figure it all out, to no avail. I think Daniel must've discovered something. Daniel was always like that. Always smart, astute. He was one of the best."

Elise swiped a hair away from between her eyes as

the wind rushed over them again. "He was. His death was a great loss to the SEAL community."

"Not just to the SEAL community, but to the world —even if the world never knows it."

His words brought a balm-like comfort to the ragged edges of her soul. "You're right. I suppose those complexities come with the job, huh?"

"Daniel didn't deserve the firestorm after his death. I know he's dead and he's not alive to see it. But you were. You went through a lot, and I am sorry about how he was treated."

Elise's heart pounded in her ears as she remembered those horrible, horrible days.

"Thank you." But her voice sounded low and scratchy with emotions she had pushed down for too long now.

"I should get you back inside." Compassion and understanding laced Colton's tone.

"That sounds good. I guess I am more tired than I thought I was."

Before she walked back to the cottage, she gave one last glance over her shoulder. The homeless man was gone, but that didn't mean danger wasn't close. She didn't know how long she would be safe here, but she dreaded to think about what the future might hold.

WITH ELISE SETTLED in her room, Colton called an emergency meeting with Dez and Griff. Ty joined them as they met in the living room.

The last member of their team, Benjamin James, was on a mission in Virginia Beach right now. The man, a former bomb tech, was guarding a senator's daughter who was in town. He'd join them here in a couple days.

Colton explained to them the information Elise had shared.

"What do you need us to do?" Dez asked.

"There were several things in the metal box she found," Colton said. "We don't have any of the actual evidence—only photos of it."

"I'm not sure how much good photos will do." Dez tilted his head, a skeptical look on his face.

"We'll do the best we can with what we've got."

"Where are the originals?" Griff asked.

"Hidden. Elise didn't say where, and I didn't ask." Colton shifted. "Now, Griff, I want you to see if you can trace the phone number Daniel called from the burner phone."

"Will do."

Colton nodded at Dez. "Dez, I want you to try and figure out what this code means."

"I'm on it."

"Ty, if you're willing to help, I'd love for you to take these pictures and see if you can ID anyone in them."

"I'd be more than happy to."

Colton shifted again, the weight of the situation pressing on him. "I want to make a list of everybody who could be responsible. Starting now."

"I think the most logical culprit would be one of the Savages," Dez said.

"I agree," Colton said. "But it would be difficult for them to make it onto US soil."

"But it wouldn't be unheard of." Griff scowled and twirled the ever-present toothpick in his mouth.

"True," Colton said. "But let's keep thinking."

"We've always suspected that an American was helping to finance them," Dez said. "Maybe Daniel discovered who it was, and this person sent his men out to get Elise."

Colton swallowed hard at the thought. He hated thinking about Elise getting caught in the crosshairs of all this. But it was reality, and he needed to deal with it.

"How about a mole on the inside at command?" Griff's cold gaze drifted from person to person. "Everyone blamed Daniel. But what if it was someone else?"

Colton's stomach clenched. That's what he'd been thinking. "None of this happened until Elise went to the command and shared what she found."

"Who was there?" Dez asked.

"Just Secretary of the Navy Stabler and Commander Larson."

Griff grunted. That summed up the situation perfectly. None of them wanted to think either of those men might be dirty. On top of that, Secretary Stabler was Benjamin's uncle.

All in all, Colton didn't like any of those possibilities.

"What about our other assignments for Blackout?" Dez asked.

"This is priority," Colton said. "But we have commitments. Until it's time for your specific assignment, let's focus on figuring out who is behind this. It's not just Elise who's in danger. It's this island. And maybe even this country."

CHAPTER NINE

ELISE WAS grateful for some time alone. Something about being out there with Colton had stirred too many memories.

Maybe it was just feeling his touch. It had brought flashes in time, flashes of when she and Daniel had been so happy.

She sat on the edge of her bed and tried to control her thoughts. But it was too late. Flashbacks of the day she'd learned about her husband's death slammed into her mind.

Elise had just gotten home from work. Her day at the office had been a particularly grueling one as she tried to deal with people who had some pretty severe issues. She knew as a psychologist that she couldn't take on her patients' problems. But seeing people self-destruct was difficult, to say the least.

She'd kicked off her shoes, turned on her favorite Taylor Swift album—it was her guilty pleasure—and went into the kitchen to begin cooking some stir-fry. Maybe she would watch a movie and start a fire to relax tonight. She needed to do something to unwind.

She had gotten used to doing things on her own. Sometimes, she didn't even feel like she was married at all. She and Daniel had been apart for more of their marriage than they had been together. It was the reality of life being married to a Navy SEAL.

Before she started to cook, a knock sounded at her door. Elise assumed it was one of her neighbors. Maybe Ernie had accidentally gotten her mail, or maybe it was the Smiths wanting to let her know they would be going out of town.

As soon as Elise opened the door and saw Colton and Dez's faces, she knew something was wrong.

"Where's Daniel?" Her voice had come out low, cautious. Hope still lingered in the back of Elise's mind, hope that she was reading too much into this situation. But she knew she wasn't.

"I am so sorry, Elise." Colton's voice cracked with emotion, and his eyes conveyed sorrow that words couldn't express.

He didn't have to say anything else. She knew.

The next instant, Colton held her as sobs escaped from the sacred places of her soul. The team had been doing training exercises when a horrible accident occurred. Daniel had been swept away by the ocean, and they hadn't been able to locate his body.

It had been four days, and the higher-ups had suspended the search.

Daniel was presumed dead.

It didn't matter that she and Daniel had been having problems. He had been her husband, and she'd loved him. A part of her had died that day along with Daniel.

To make matters worse, their last conversation had been more of a fight.

"I don't know if I can do this anymore," she'd told Daniel as they stood at the door.

He'd worn his uniform and had a duffle bag slung over his shoulder. He'd always kept his dark hair short —no fuss, as he liked to say.

Daniel also liked to say, when talking about the SEALs, that for the team to work they had to have some members who could carry a house and others who could run around the house.

In other words, they needed both strength and speed. Burly guys weren't as fast as the leaner ones, and the leaner ones didn't have the bulk to muscle through certain situations.

Daniel had been strong but lean. On the outside, he'd been fit and hard. But on the inside, he had a soft, compassionate side.

At least, he had until the months leading up to his death.

"Don't say that." His eyes had pleaded with her. "We'll talk about it more when I get back, okay?"

Elise hadn't said anything more.

As Daniel had walked out the door, his expression was nothing less than heartbroken. She'd had the power to take that away, to make things right. Yet she hadn't.

Bitterness had begun to set in. When Daniel got back, he was going to have to make a choice: stay married or remain a SEAL. He couldn't do both.

Elise hadn't wanted to whine, but she felt alone. Neglected. Sometimes, she felt like she was living with a stranger. She envied her friends who went on dates and trips with their spouses. Who had someone to help out at home.

She wanted kids, but how could she bring a child into the world knowing she'd practically be a single mom?

She didn't want to give up on her marriage. But something needed to change.

Colton and Dez had stayed by her side for the next three hours until Elise's best friend could come over and stay with her that night.

Elise had seen the grief and worry in Colton's eyes as well. This hadn't affected only her. Colton was going through a firestorm of grief and loss.

The next few days had been awful as Elise tried to figure out the next steps.

Right when she thought things couldn't get worse, Commander Larson had shown up. The man was a decorated war hero with hair that had grayed at the sides. He wasn't a necessarily big man, but he carried himself like a giant. He spoke with authority, and every action seemed purposeful. He'd almost been like a father figure to her.

He'd wanted to tell her in person that they discovered a secret banking account Daniel had set up. The transactions there, which were worth almost one million, could be traced back to the Savages.

Elise couldn't believe her ears. She'd adamantly denied that Daniel would do something like that to her and to his country.

She'd then learned that the government had suspected a traitor was feeding information to the terrorist group. They believed that person was Daniel.

Everything around Elise had faded as his words echoed in her mind, each reverberation hitting her like a hammer to the head. "I don't believe it, and I never will. I can't believe that you're even considering it."

Commander Larson had frowned before showing her a video of Daniel at that bank on the day the account had been set up. It seemed irrefutable proof. But Elise still didn't buy it. There had to be an explanation.

Larson had also shown her a picture of Daniel meeting with someone named Tara Campbell. The woman had worked for the CIA but was also believed to have ties with the Savages, the commander explained. She'd been killed a week before Daniel while in a conflict in Kabul, Afghanistan. Larson believed she and Daniel were working together and that both were receiving kickbacks for the information they provided.

Those had been some of the worst days of Elise's life. Nausea still roiled in her stomach when she thought about it.

A year later, she still didn't have answers. She had no idea what was going on. But she knew that there was no way Daniel was guilty of doing those things. She needed to find out the truth and clear her husband. She'd thought that task was impossible—until she'd found that hidden box in Daniel's room.

Her only comfort had been found in knowing that Colton was in her corner.

She pulled a pillow into her lap and stared out the window at the beach. She only hoped she could find some answers—some closure—here. But she knew that the people behind this were desperate to cover up ... something.

Was she really prepared to find out what?

AT THE FIRST OPPORTUNITY, Cassidy pulled Colton and Ty aside.

She'd wanted to talk to them earlier, but she'd been caught up in a phone call with the mayor about a music festival the town's PR director was trying to plan for the spring. Even as they'd discussed some details, Cassidy had other things on her mind—things dealing with Elise's presence here.

This was her island, and Cassidy needed to know exactly what might be happening here right now. Because if this was as big as she thought it might be, it wasn't just the people here in this house in danger. It was everyone in this community.

She slipped from her bedroom and saw Ty and Colton standing near the front door talking in low tones.

Before Cassidy could bring up the subject, Colton jumped in. "You know anything about a homeless man here on the island?"

"The one who looks like Jason Momoa?" she asked.

"The Aquaman guy?" Ty raised an eyebrow in mock jealousy. "Interesting observation."

"It wasn't me. A group of ladies here on a girls' weekend were talking about it." Cassidy raised her hands in innocence. "Making it even more ironic, his name is Jason. And, by the way, you're totally my hero, so no worries, okay?"

"I wasn't worried."

"Good." Cassidy turned her hands over on the table, ready to spell out what she knew. "This Jason guy showed up here on the island about three days ago. As far as I can tell, he's harmless. But we're keeping an eye on him. Mac says he looks like trouble."

Colton nodded, his eyes focused with thought. "Do you have many homeless people here?"

"Historically, no. But Mac said we always have a few people—usually surfers—who come here and become the stereotypical beach bums. As long as they can surf, they're happy."

Mac McArthur was the former police chief, current mayor, and all-around fixture here in this town.

"But it's cold outside," Colton said. "I can't imagine wanting to live outside on this island in the winter."

"I know. Apparently, they set up little camps in the woods and sleep there at night while begging during the day or dumpster diving." Cassidy saw that Colton's eyes still looked tumultuous. "We're looking into this. I'm not saying the homeless cause trouble, but we want to have both caution and compassion. You think this guy Jason is somehow connected with Elise?"

"I don't know. I want to say no, but nothing is off the table. Elise went to the command a week ago. What if whoever is behind these attacks sent someone here—before Elise even showed up? If there's something askew, me and my guys are going to be under the microscope as well. It might be a longshot . . . but it might not be."

"Colton's right." Ty's jaw looked tight, and his voice sounded serious. "We can't take anything for granted. While I've never dealt with the Savages directly, I know enough about them to know they're vile and have no respect for human life. If they come here to this island, it's going to be trouble."

Cassidy released her breath, trying to think the logistics through. "If one of these guys—the Savages—were to come here to the island, would I be able to spot them? Do they make an effort to blend in? Do they even have people here in the US?"

"Last I heard, they've been recruiting in the US," Ty said. "If there were known terrorists within our borders, the FBI would be all over it. But these guys are smart, and they have money."

"Where do they get their money?" Cassidy asked, wiping stray crumbs from the table.

"We've suspected for a while there's someone in the US who might be financing them," Colton said. "The CIA has been trying to follow the money trail. Of course, I'm not privy to any of that information anymore."

"They hate the US more than any other group that I've ever seen." Ty glanced out the window and frowned. "And I've seen some pretty hateful groups."

She raised her eyebrows. "You'd even rank them above the Taliban?"

"Yes, I would," Ty said.

"Then why haven't I heard more about them?" Cassidy tried to put the pieces together. Something just didn't seem to fit. She watched the news every morning, and she'd heard very little about the group. Why wasn't their name all over the headlines?

"Word of them hasn't spread through the media yet," Colton said. "The government has been trying to keep them under wraps so as to not cause hysteria. But it's only a matter of time before people learn more. Their attacks are growing more violent, and they're becoming harder to ignore."

Cassidy leaned back and frowned. "I don't like the sound of this."

It seemed like every time they had a few months of peace and quiet here on the island, something else happened. And it was never something small. First, a ruthless West Coast gang had come here. Then Gilead's Cove, a deadly cult, had moved onto the island. Their little beach town just couldn't seem to catch a break.

Colton's gaze met hers. "Me and my guys are here to help you in whatever way we can."

Cassidy leaned back and nodded. In the eight or nine months since she had gotten to know Colton, she'd been nothing but impressed. He was a good guy, and Ty trusted him. That went a long way for her. The rest of the team seemed equally as honorable.

Cassidy glanced at her watch. "Unfortunately, I've got to go to my meeting now, but I'll keep my eyes open. Let's have open communication going here. I'll let you know if I see trouble, and you do the same for me."

"I will," Colton said.

Ty stood. "I'll walk you out."

He placed a hand on her back and stepped onto the screened-in porch. They silently walked down the stairs, Kujo on their heels. A brisk wind swept over them, and the salty ocean scent reminded her that she was just a small part of a bigger plan. The beach—and even just living here in Lantern Beach—reminded her of that fact daily.

It was one more reason she loved being here. It helped keep her life in perspective.

Ty paused beside her police cruiser. "Are you really okay with this? When I told you I wanted to start Hope House, you may have never imagined taking on all of this."

"It sounds like your friends need help. That's what we're here for. I just don't want to see other innocent people get hurt in the process."

"Neither do I." Ty pushed the hair out of her eyes as wind swept around them. "Neither do any of us."

Her heart pounded at her husband's touch. She

hoped that feeling never went away. She thanked God every day for sending Ty into her life. "Be safe."

Ty leaned forward and planted a kiss on her lips. "I will, and you too."

"I pray this meeting doesn't end in a fistfight." Cassidy wished she was joking, but there had been so much tension over this possible hotel that she had no idea what to expect tonight. Her only comfort was in knowing that Mayor Mac MacArthur would also be there to help her take some of the heat.

Chaos was trying to return to her island. Cassidy could feel it in her bones. She was going to do everything in her power to stop that from happening.

CHAPTER TEN

COLTON HAD ESCAPED to his cabana for the evening. There were six behind the house and each was a different beachy color—coral, yellow, turquoise, navy blue, purple, and pink. The places were small but ample, with a double bed, a tiny bathroom, an efficiency kitchen, and two chairs with a table. A small loft filled the space near the ceiling. Outside, each of them had a small porch with a hammock.

Colton and his guys were only staying here temporarily until they could figure out something more permanent. But the setup was perfect for them.

He'd just opened a bottle of water when he heard a knock at the door. He grabbed his gun and stepped closer, knowing he needed to stay on guard. As he peered out the window, he saw Dez standing there. He placed his gun back on the table before opening the door and ushering his friend side.

"I found out something I knew you would want to know." Dez held up some papers.

Colton pointed to the chair in the corner and motioned for him to sit down. While he lowered himself into the matching chair across from Dez, Colton's heart pounded with anticipation of what he might learn.

"What's going on?" he asked.

"So I've been staring at these numbers and letters that Elise found. I definitely think this is some type of code, but it's top level. I have a couple programs that can usually break things like this."

"So you had no luck decoding this one?"

"Not yet," Dez said. "It's beyond the scope of my computer program. But I think I know someone who can. Kari Stevenson."

"I remember Kari. She's one of the top cryptologists in the country."

Dez nodded. "That's right. I know her personally. I know that we can trust her."

Colton didn't feel quite as certain, for more than one reason—starting with the fact that he didn't know whom he could trust right now. "I don't know if I want to bring someone else into this."

"I'm telling you, I've been working on this for hours and I've gotten nowhere. If we want to know what this says, we're going to need help. You can trust Kari."

"It's not so much that I'm afraid we can't trust her. It's more the fact that I don't know if we should pull anyone else into this."

"You're afraid that she would be in danger." Dez's lips pulled down in a frown.

"Exactly."

"I could apprise her of the potential consequences of this, and she could have the chance to agree or disagree. That way, she'd be going in with her eyes wide open if she decided to help."

Colton nodded. "I like that idea better. But we're also going to need a cover story. As much as I want to think we can trust everyone, somebody is working for the other side."

Dez rubbed the tattoo on his forearm, the one that looked like a rosary, as he muttered, "You really think so?"

"I really think so." Colton stroked his jaw as it began to throb. He'd been gritting his teeth today, and he knew it. It happened whenever he had a lot on his mind.

"It's your call." Dez raised his head, the action showing he still had respect for the chain of command, even though they were no longer in the military. "I'll do whatever you want."

Colton chewed on it for only a minute before

saying, "Talk to Kari. Use the secure line in the office, just to be safe. If Kari doesn't want to help, we won't pressure her."

"I'll do that."

Colton shook his head, still thinking about Dez's discovery. "A military code, huh?"

"What's that look for?"

"There's only a small circle of people who could be responsible." His gaze met Dez's. "Someone we know has betrayed us."

"Who knows about that last mission besides the five of us?" Dez leaned forward in his chair, his gaze narrow with thought.

Colton had been thinking about it all day, ever since Elise had shown up. Worst-case scenarios continued to run through his mind. "Let's start at the top. The Secretary of the Navy authorized the operation."

"But he didn't necessarily know the details." Dez tapped his fingers together. "He probably got some intel from a CIA operative and knew we needed to act."

"Again, the CIA operative probably didn't know the details of what we were going to do. They were just passing along information."

Dez nodded. "Correct. Commander Larson was then handed the intel, and he helped to plan the operation. He pulled us into it once the details were finalized."

Colton pressed his teeth together, reminding himself not to grind them. He pictured that meeting leading up to their mission. "The commander's assistant was also there when we were debriefed. He didn't necessarily know when it was taking place, but he was aware of what we were going to do."

"True. And we can't forget Beanie. He drove the boat to take us to the site. He's still in the service. Stationed in the Middle East right now, so I think we can rule him out."

Colton's thoughts shifted to Benjamin again. He hated to think one of his men could be responsible. But Benjamin was less bonded with the team. He'd been the newest SEAL to join them. He kept to himself, and something about the man made him hard to get to know.

"What are you thinking?" Dez studied Colton's face a moment.

"Nothing worth sharing." Getting something like that out in the open would only spell trouble. But if one of his men had betrayed them, it was better to keep that person close, to keep an eye on him.

Dez stood but paused, something still obviously on his mind. "I can't believe Elise is back."

When he heard Dez say her name, something clenched inside Colton. Benjamin was supposed to be keeping an eye on Daniel when everything went wrong. Though he didn't blame Benjamin, part of

Colton wondered how things would be different right now if Benjamin had done his job properly.

Colton had tried to forget that thought for the past year, but it was nearly impossible. Almost every day, Colton reviewed the facts of their last operation. He tried to figure out what could have been done to ensure Daniel was still with them now.

Things would be so different if he was. Daniel would be here to defend himself, to tell people that he wasn't guilty of the things he'd been accused of. Maybe Colton and all his guys would still be SEALs.

It was unsettling how just one day could change everything. But that's what had happened. Nothing had been the same since that mission went south.

"Does Elise know the truth?" Dez asked.

"No." Colton's throat tightened as he said the word.

"You going to tell her?"

"I don't know yet. It's classified. But Daniel was her husband. And if she knows all the details..."

"She won't blame you. It wasn't your fault."

Colton said nothing. But he knew it was his fault. No one would change his mind.

And if Elise found out the truth, she'd never forgive him.

Dez left a few minutes later, and Colton locked the door behind him. But he couldn't bring himself to sit back down. His muscles were too rigid and tight. Instead, he stood by a window and stared outside.

If it was any other night, he would go out for a jog or lift weights. But he didn't want to wander too far away from the house where Elise stayed. Though he knew she was in good hands there with Ty and Cassidy, Colton still felt responsible for her.

Daniel would want him to keep an eye on her. He'd hate to know how his death had shattered Elise's heart.

Before Colton dropped the curtain, he saw something move near the sand dunes in the distance.

He tensed.

Someone was out there, he realized.

Whoever it was, Colton couldn't let him get away.

He grabbed his gun and reached for the door.

CHAPTER ELEVEN

COLTON WAS thankful he wore black joggers and a long-sleeved black T-shirt. It would help him blend into the night.

He jogged around the cabana toward the sand dunes in the distance.

Who was out there? Was it the same person who had attacked Elise at her home last night?

Anger burned up his spine at the thought. That person deserved to pay. If Elise hadn't been so sharp, she'd be dead right now.

The sand muted the sound of Colton's steps. The half-moon tonight offered a scattering of light, but still enough dimness to conceal him.

He paused near a low-lying shrub and glanced around. Where had the shadow gone?

Colton had definitely seen movement over here,

and it wasn't just the marsh grass swaying in the breeze. Someone had been crouching there.

On silent footsteps, he moved toward the spot. Everything was quiet around him except for the occasional breeze rustling the dry foliage.

Ty's place was fairly secluded with no houses on the north side, only a wide stretch of marsh. On the other side was another cottage, which was empty right now.

Colton held his gun steady, listening for the sound of someone sneaking up on him.

He still heard nothing.

Finally, he reached the area where he'd seen the shadow. The man had been behind a patch of seagrass. Now the site was empty.

But footprints imprinted the ground.

Colton definitely hadn't been imagining things. Someone had most definitely been here.

He glanced around again. Still no one.

The bad feeling grew in his gut. The fact that this person had managed to evade Colton showed he knew what he was doing. Maybe he was even a professional.

Remaining low, Colton traced the footprints, but the tracks ended at the marsh grass.

What was on the other side of this area?

Just as the question entered his mind, an engine roared to life.

Colton popped his head up in time to see headlights speeding away in the distance.

Someone had been here, but they'd gotten away. Colton knew there was no chance of catching this person now. By the time he hopped in his car, this guy would be long gone.

But his worry only continued to snowball. Whatever was going on, Colton feared somebody would get hurt before it was all done.

He vowed that person wouldn't be Elise.

CHAPTER TWELVE

ELISE AWOKE the next morning from a restless night. Bad dreams had plagued her—dreams of someone breaking into her room. Except, in her dreams, she'd given the information over before the man shot her. She'd woken up before the bullet could pierce her skin.

The sequences felt so real that her mind reeled with revulsion.

Finally, she got dressed and followed the sound of sizzling food into the kitchen. Cassidy stood at the counter, cooking some bacon and pancakes.

"Morning," Elise called.

Cassidy glanced over her shoulder. "Good morning."

"Let me help. I'm a great pancake maker."

"I won't argue with having some assistance." Cassidy handed over her spatula.

"You always cook for the guys?" She took her place by the griddle, thankful for a moment of normalcy.

Cassidy let out a short laugh. "Nope. I'm feeling generous today. And I haven't gotten any calls yet. Usually, the guys take turns."

"Nice." Elise glanced around. "Speaking of which, where is everyone right now?"

"Working out. They jog on the beach every morning and then lift weights. They have to stay in shape if they're going to do their jobs."

"I suppose they do."

"They let me join them sometimes. I think they're afraid I'm going to outdo them, though." She flashed a smile.

Elise smiled back. She'd always appreciated any woman who could put a SEAL in his place—especially if they didn't take themselves too seriously about it. Cassidy seemed perfect for the job.

"Any updates on my car?" Elise asked, taking her place at the counter.

Cassidy's smile disappeared. "As a matter of fact, yes. A bomb was positioned on the undercarriage of the vehicle. It appears to have been detonated with a cell phone."

"Someone could do that remotely?"

She nodded. "Yes, they could."

"So, for all they knew, I could have been in the car?"

"Maybe. But you also need to remember that, with that cell phone, they could have tracked your location. The explosion going off when it did could have just been a means of sending a message."

Elise felt herself wobble as she stood there at the counter.

"The good news is that you're safe—for now." Cassidy flashed a comforting smile before flipping a piece of bacon. "By the way, Ty only had good things to say about Daniel. He called him a true American hero."

"He was a good man."

"If you don't mind me asking, how did the two of you meet? Were you high school sweethearts?"

"No, I don't mind at all. As a matter of fact, we *were* high school sweethearts." Those days seemed like another lifetime ago. "Daniel was captain of the debate team. I was president of the school's service club. We had to team up to do a project—the school's idea, not ours. We couldn't have been less thrilled to work with each other. But once we really got to know each other, we were both smitten. I knew he was the one for me."

Cassidy raised her eyebrows. "Is that right? That's great. How long were you guys married?"

Elise flipped some pancakes that had turned golden brown. "We dated for three years, we were engaged six months, and we were married for nearly a decade."

"I'm really sorry to hear about what happened to him."

Elise nodded solemnly. "Thank you. It was a shock to all of us, to say the least."

"I guess you met the rest of the gang because of your husband."

"Yes, I did. He and Colton were really great friends. They met at BUD/S."

"Colton's a great guy. I've really enjoyed getting to know him. All of the guys, really. But I've known Colton the longest." Cassidy turned another piece of bacon.

"Yes, there's something about Colton that you just don't forget, do you?"

"Are you talking about his biceps?" Cassidy raised her eyebrows. "Don't get me wrong, I'm a married woman. A very happily married woman. But nobody can miss those muscles."

Elise chuckled, feeling her cheeks flush. "It is one of his finer qualities, but certainly not his only one."

"No, certainly not."

Elise sobered again. "Colton really was there for me after Daniel died. I guess I felt like he was the only one who really understood what it was like to lose Daniel. We were the two closest to him, I suppose."

Cassidy offered a sympathetic smile. "I could see where that would have bonded the two of you. And now he's like a big brother?" Cassidy looked at her.

Was there more to the look in her eyes? Was she trying to feel Elise out to see if she was interested in Colton? Because that thought was ridiculous.

"Yes, kind of like a big brother."

"Well, it's always good to have a big brother to watch out for you." Cassidy put the remaining bacon on a platter—and just in time.

The door opened, and Colton stepped inside. Elise felt herself suck in a quick breath.

Her reaction made no sense. It was like yesterday when he had touched her shoulder and electricity jolted through her body. There was no reason for that. Colton had always been her friend, and that's all they would ever be. That's all they *could* ever be.

His face seemed to soften when he spotted Elise, and something resembling a smile tugged at his lips.

"Morning," he called, stepping closer. "The rest of the gang is coming in a few minutes. They're getting cleaned up."

"Good morning." Elise let the last batch of pancakes cook and grabbed a mug from the cabinet. "Can I get you some coffee?"

"I'd love some."

Something about the way he said the words made Elise think he hadn't gotten much sleep last night. Why was that? Had something else happened?

If so, certainly he would tell her.

She poured a cup for him and set it on the table before finishing up the pancakes.

Colton glanced at Cassidy. "How did your meeting go last night?"

Cassidy frowned. "Not well. There were some very heated emotions."

"People really don't want this hotel going in, do they?" Colton asked.

"No, they most certainly do not. I don't envy the position that Mac is in right now. If only standards had been put in place before all this happened, it wouldn't be an issue right now. But what we're dealing with is the will of the people versus the development of the island. I can really see the positives and negatives for both. But it's going to be an ugly fight."

Colton grunted. "Politics are never fun."

"You can say that again."

Colton shifted and ran a hand over his hair. There was something on his mind, Elise realized.

"Did something else happen?" Elise finally asked.

Colton remained quiet a moment, his eyes narrowing with obvious displeasure. Finally, he said, "There was someone outside last night. I tried to follow him, but he got into a car and got away before I could catch him."

Elise gasped. "What?"

He nodded. "Somebody appeared to be scoping out the place."

"Does Ty know?" Cassidy's eyebrows knit together.

"I texted him last night. It was late. You were probably already asleep."

"I need to know these things." Cassidy's voice sounded pointed and stern.

Colton nodded. "I know. That's what I came over here this morning to tell you."

Elise crossed her arms over her chest. If her tormentor already knew she was here, that didn't leave her much time to figure things out.

But there was nowhere she could go where she'd be safe. So what was she supposed to do? All Elise could do was stand her ground.

That's what Daniel would have told her.

COLTON'S GUT jostled with unease. He didn't like this any more than anyone else. He had stayed awake for most of the night, watching for any signs that trouble had returned. He'd seen nothing, but he couldn't let his guard down.

He'd do whatever it took to keep Elise safe.

The door behind them opened, and Griff stepped inside. He nodded at everyone, never one for small talk. Instead, he walked over to the table, where Colton and Elise sat with Ty and Cassidy, and frowned.

"I heard an update on the fire at your place, Elise," he announced. "I've been keeping my eye on it."

"And?" Colton asked.

"It was caused by a gas line explosion."

Elise's gaze fixated on Griff, and she looked like she was barely breathing. "What about the body inside?"

Griff frowned again. "The body they found inside was a male. Still unidentified. There was a bullet wound to his chest."

"A bullet wound? My gun . . . I left it there. It fell from my hand when the man grabbed me. What if . . .?" Her words came out fast, almost panicked.

"If that was the gun used in the crime?" Colton finished. "It's a possibility."

"The police are trying to locate Elise to ask her more questions," Griff continued.

"What should I do?" Elise glanced around the table. "Should I call them?"

"I know this will go against everything your instincts are telling you, but the less people who know where you are, the better," Colton said.

"I agree," Ty said. "There's a good chance someone already knows you're here. But, just in case, we don't want to tip them off."

"What if the police think I did something wrong?" Elise nearly sounded breathless. She reached into her pocket and pulled out her phone. She was thinking about calling the authorities, wasn't she? Thinking about telling them what was going on.

"Let's just let this play out a little longer," Colton urged. Until they knew whom they could trust, they needed to keep their circle small.

Elise stared at him a moment, part of her bottom lip tucked into her mouth as she nibbled on it. Colton knew she had a big decision to make, and he hoped she would listen to his advice.

"If you think so," she said. "I'll wait. For a little while, at least."

He released his breath.

Good. They needed all the time they could buy themselves to find some answers.

They heard a ping, and Elise glanced at her screen again. Then her face went pale.

"What is it?" Colton leaned closer.

Her wide eyes met his. "I got another threat."

"What do you mean another threat?"

She showed him the screen. The words there were stark and clear.

Turn over the information or we go public with your indiscretions.

Below that was a picture of Elise facing a man, both

smiling at each other as the darkness stretched behind them.

There was obviously more to this picture than Colton realized. He only knew that seeing Elise smile at somebody like that did something to his heart that it shouldn't.

CHAPTER THIRTEEN

ELISE FELT her stomach drop as she sagged against the table. She couldn't believe this was happening, but it was.

"Elise?" Colton stared at her as if waiting for an explanation.

Explaining this was the last thing she wanted to do, though. Instead, she rubbed her brow as she felt a tension headache coming on.

"Elise?" Colton repeated.

She let out a long breath before dragging her gaze back up to meet his. "It's not what it looks like."

"I'm not even sure what this looks like. You went on a date? That doesn't seem to be all that bad."

"No, I didn't go on a date," she said. "I ran into that man while I was doing some errands. He gave me a hug, and somebody must've snapped that picture."

"I'm still not following." Colton shook his head and waited patiently for her to explain.

She lowered her eyelids again before raising her gaze to meet his. "Colton, that man is one of my patients. He started making me uncomfortable, so I told my secretary he was going to have to find a new psychologist."

"What do you mean by uncomfortable?" Cassidy pushed her plate away, her full attention on Elise.

Elise frowned and let out a long breath. "I mean, he kept coming on to me. He would tell me how he had dreams about me. That if he only had someone like me in his life then he would be happy. He went through these manic episodes where he thought he could conquer the world."

"Okay." Colton squinted. "So let me get this straight. This man came onto you, you were about to recommend him to a different psychologist, and then you happen to run into him out in public and someone snapped this picture?"

"Yes, that's what happened. But this photo makes it look like more, doesn't it?" Elise frowned again and shook her head.

Colton looked at the picture again. "It does look like the two of you were out for the evening together."

"Colton, in my line of work I cannot have a personal relationship with my patients. Things like that are reason to lose my license."

"This picture isn't enough to prove anything," he said.

"I have a feeling this is the tip of the iceberg."

"So you think someone set you up?" Cassidy asked.

Elise shrugged. "That's my best guess. I knew that something felt off about this man. I even said something to one of my colleagues about it. But I haven't felt like myself for this past year, and sometimes, with that, I've doubted my own feelings. That was obviously a mistake."

"This one picture alone shouldn't be enough for the board to take away your license," Colton said. "Do you think whoever is behind this will plant other evidence?"

"That's what my gut tells me," Elise said. "If whoever is behind this has gone as far as to plant a fake patient within my practice, then who's to say they haven't gone as far as to fabricate other evidence?"

Colton frowned.

His feelings seemed to match Elise's. She knew if someone had already gone to these extremes, they likely had other things up their sleeve.

She had to figure out who might be behind this. There was no time to waste.

ELISE SAT in a chair by the window with a cup of

coffee in hand. The rest of the gang had split up to do their respective tasks, and Elise had been left alone with her thoughts.

She couldn't escape the headache that haunted her since she got that text. She had to make the choice between giving up what could be critical intel or losing the career she had worked so hard to build.

Her psychology practice had gotten her through her days since Daniel died. Helping other people become better versions of themselves had been rewarding. It made her feel like she was making a difference.

It also made her forget about her own problems.

She supposed, in her own way, she had used her busyness as a healing tool since Daniel's death. As long as she had too many things to do, she couldn't stop long enough to think about her loss.

And this was why.

Breakfast was three hours ago. They'd eaten and cleaned up, and now Elise had nothing to do. She was miserable. All she could do was sit here and think about her choice.

But she knew there was no choice. She could never choose herself over national security. How could she? These guys who were here, the members of Blackout, had been willing to give up their lives for their country. She couldn't even consider placing her career over the greater good.

Despite that realization, the thought still weighed heavily on her. These evil people were trying to ruin her life, and they were coming close to succeeding. If only she could do something else that might help catch them. But, right now, there was little else she could do except try to remain safe.

If Elise protected herself, she could protect the information. That's what she kept telling herself, at least.

"Hey, you." Colton stood from the kitchen table where he'd been reviewing some notes he'd made and wandered toward her. That familiar look of worry stained his face as he lowered himself into the seat across from Elise. "What are you thinking about?"

She shrugged and took another sip of her coffee. Mostly she'd been staring out the window at the gray day outside. For a while, she'd even tried to imagine that it was summertime and that she was in Lantern Beach on a relaxing vacation. That trick only worked for a few minutes before reality came crashing back.

"I just can't believe all of this is happening. I thought the worst was over. Daniel was dead. People thought he was a traitor. How could it get much darker? But it has."

Colton leaned closer. "We're going to get through this. I don't know how. I don't know what's going to happen. But we're going to be right here by your side."

She reached forward and squeezed his hand. "I really appreciate that, Colton. It means a lot to me."

She pulled her hand back into her lap, reminded again of the electricity she felt whenever she and Colton touched. Another round of guilt pummeled her. If she was smart, she would make sure she never touched Colton again. The feelings it produced could never come to fruition.

"Listen, how about if we grab a bite to eat?" Colton suggested.

Her gaze met his, and she didn't bother to hide her skepticism. "Is that safe?"

"The guys are going. We'll be there with you. I know you well enough to know that you're going to be miserable if you have to stay cooped inside until this is resolved. You can go out. You're just going to have several escorts who are keeping an eye on you."

"Makes me feel kind of important." She tried to smile.

Colton stooped down until their eyes met again. "You are important, Elise. You always have been, even before all of this happened."

His words caused a burst of warmth to explode inside her.

But her smile disappeared as she remembered the earlier threat she'd received. "It just seems like such a nightmare."

"Did you decide what you're going to do?"

She shuddered. "I have no doubt that this person would go as far as to kill me to get the information he wants. But I'm not going to hand it over."

Colton swallowed so hard his neck visibly tightened. "You do realize that this could escalate, right? This person will start with your career, and then move on from there."

"I know."

"Elise..." Colton's voice sounded concerned.

She shook her head. "It's already decided. I've got to do what's best for everyone, not just myself."

He stared at her another moment before nodding. "I know that's what you decided, but maybe part of me hoped it would be different."

"I wish I could be, Colton. I wish I could be." Her voice cracked.

But she couldn't compromise, not when the well-being of others was on the line.

CHAPTER FOURTEEN

COLTON'S GAZE scanned the street in front of him as he headed to the restaurant. He'd been on guard all morning, but he hadn't seen anything that registered as dangerous. Whoever had been there last night appeared to be long gone.

Dez and Griff followed behind them in another car, and Ty drove his vintage truck at the lead. Was it overkill? Some people might think so. But Colton didn't want to take any chances.

Elise was right. Whoever was trying to get this information would stop at nothing to do so. Though he hated to hear that she wasn't going to give it up, another part of him admired her even more for her stance. Her decision was selfless. Then again, that didn't surprise Colton. He'd always known that about her.

Since Benjamin was in Virginia Beach already, Colton had asked him to talk to Tara Campbell's boyfriend. She was the CIA handler who'd died around the same time as Daniel. Maybe Benjamin would be able to get some information from him. Colton hoped so.

"So, where are we going?" Elise asked, the brightness still not returning to her voice.

"It's called The Crazy Chefette. Our good friend Lisa runs it, along with her husband, Braden. Do you remember Braden Dillinger? I think you may have met a couple times. He was special forces."

"The name sounds familiar. I didn't realize so many of you guys had come out here."

"We owe that to Ty. He used to come to Lantern Beach as a child, and he ended up moving here after he got out of the military. He's our connection."

"It sounds like he's doing good work, and so are you." She sent an encouraging smile his way.

Every time Elise smiled at him, everything in Colton's world felt right. Even if it was just for a few seconds, it was still better than nothing. But that feeling was dangerous. The safest bet was to feel nothing at all.

"I think you'll like this place. Lisa is always great at putting together unexpected flavor combinations. At first, I thought it was kind of froufrou, but I've grown to appreciate her recipes. I think you will too."

"I look forward to trying them then." Elise sighed, and a new heaviness seemed to settle on her as she shifted beside him. "I know I've already said this, but I'm sorry for bringing you into this."

"You didn't bring me into anything, Elise. In fact, if anything, you were the one I dragged into this whole situation. You didn't sign up for any of this."

"I suppose I did when I married Daniel."

"All he wanted was to keep you safe."

"I know he did." Her voice trailed off with grief.

"I am sorry about everything you've gone through over the past year." Colton truly was. Every time he saw her tears, it was enough to break him.

"This isn't the way I saw my future with Daniel going. But it's like I tell my patients, there are very few things we're promised in this life. The best thing that we can do for ourselves is to be grateful for the circumstances we have, to find whatever light we can in what might seem like complete darkness."

"That sounds like great advice."

"It's true advice too. A grateful heart can go a long way. The challenge is because sometimes we want to live in the past, especially when we've lost things important to us and they remain in that space."

They pulled to a stop in front of a cheerful restaurant with yellow painted bricks and pink shutters. The sign on the outside read "The Crazy Chefette" and featured a cartoonish image of a blonde woman in a lab coat holding a beaker in one hand and a spatula in the other. Under the business name were the words "Mad Food Created by a Crazy Woman."

Colton climbed out and came around to her door. As Elise stepped into the frigid winter air, she glanced around.

Was her attacker here? Was he watching, waiting for the right opportunity to pounce?

Her throat tightened at the thought.

But as Colton's arm brushed hers, she remembered that her temporary protector was here, sheltering her. She knew without a doubt Colton would give his life to keep her safe. That was an attribute she was more than grateful for.

Elise just hated the fact she'd put him in danger. If something happened to him or his team, she'd never forgive herself.

SOMEHOW COLTON and Elise ended up in a booth by themselves while Dez, Griff, and Ty sat in another booth behind them. The place was full, and there were no tables big enough for all of them. It was just as well. Colton would never complain about having more time to talk to Elise alone.

After they ordered their drinks—sweet tea for both

of them—Elise glanced around the restaurant and gave an approving nod. "This is cute. I like it."

Satisfaction stretched through him, compounded by the alluring scent of Old Bay and sizzling homemade potato chips. "I thought you might. Grilled cheese and peaches are Lisa's specialty, but anything you order will be good."

"I have to admit I'm in the mood for some comfort food. Roast beef and mashed potatoes? Check, check." She leaned toward the menu and squinted. "Actually, that's roast beef with dried fruit, applesauce, and siracha."

"You'll like it." Colton winked. "I promise. Lisa hasn't let me down yet."

"Then I'm going to trust you on that." Elise closed her menu and glanced around the restaurant again. "It just seems so surreal to be here right now."

"It seems surreal to me that you're here."

"It is like old times, huh?" She tilted her head, a nostalgic look in her gaze. "I thought this chapter of my life was permanently closed."

Colton wanted to say that it was. That she was safe and free to be happy. But he'd be lying if he told her that.

Still, he had to admit that there was something about being with Elise that felt very familiar. But, in the past, Daniel had always been there. Colton had been the third wheel, the odd man out. But Elise had never made him feel that way.

A piece of their trifecta was missing, and the loss would always remain.

Colton watched as two ladies walked past, their eyes lingering on Dez. Elise followed his gaze and raised her eyebrows.

"He always gets that reaction." Colton smiled. "We always tell him it's his eyes."

Elise grinned. "His eyes, huh?"

"He flirts without ever saying a word. It's his superpower."

Elise chuckled. "Dez does have a bit of a playboy vibe."

"I wouldn't know about that, but I did hear that his high school class voted him least likely to ever get married."

Elise shook her head, her chuckles fading. "That's terrible."

"I didn't say it was because nobody *wanted* to marry him. It's just that Dez has an aversion to settling down."

"I see what you're saying." Her gaze shifted. "How about Griff? What's going on with him? I still keep up with Bethany on occasion. She hasn't seemed the same since Griff left."

Bethany was Griff's ex-wife. The two had split a year ago—right after Daniel died. To say the divorce had been hard on Bethany would be an understatement. There were still so many unanswered questions. To make it worse, their daughter, Ada, was only three.

"He doesn't really talk about it a lot. He still claims the divorce was what he wanted, but I feel like there's more to his story."

Elise swirled her ice using a paper straw, the liquid stirring along with her thoughts. "I could tell that he loved his wife and daughter more than anything. I just can't believe they're not together anymore. Neither can Bethany."

"We were all shocked, and Griff hasn't been the same since. I figure when he's ready to talk about it, he will."

Elise nodded somberly. "Let's hope."

Colton let out a sigh before shifting the subject again. "And then there's Benjamin, who's working an assignment up in Virginia Beach. He has that boyish look about him sometimes, the one that makes everyone feel like he's their best friend."

"I can see that."

"Out of everyone here, he's probably the one I know the least. Griff is quiet, but when he opens up, he won't hold back on letting you know how he feels. Benjamin, on the other hand . . . he has things going on behind those eyes, things I have trouble getting a read on. He's friends with everyone, but only at the surface level, you know?"

"He's protecting himself for some reason," Elise

said.

Was he protecting himself because he had secrets from the rest of them? Colton pushed the thought aside. He hated doubting anyone on his team. But sometimes it was the smart thing to do.

"Are he and Griff still a team?" Elise asked. "I remember Daniel saying that Griff was almost like a mentor to Benjamin."

"The two have a good relationship. Griff is good for Benjamin."

"It's always nice to have someone like that in your life." Elise shifted. "It's great that you're all so different yet you get along together so well."

Colton said nothing, determined not to give away his doubts. Saying them aloud would do nothing to help the situation.

The waitress took their order, then Colton and Elise settled back to wait for their food. Before they could start up another conversation, Cassidy walked in. She stopped by the other table first before sliding into the empty seat next to Elise.

"I'm not staying for long," Cassidy started. "I'm just picking up something to eat, and I happened to see you all here."

"How's it going today?" Elise asked.

Cassidy nodded at someone across the restaurant.

"You see that man over there? His name is Damien Marks. He's the developer who wants to build the hotel. Apparently, someone went to his rental house last night and spray-painted it and smashed the windshield on his Mercedes."

"Wow," Colton said. "You're right when you say people feel strongly about this hotel."

"I think it's made him only more determined to get this deal done."

Colton looked at the man again. The fifty-something man had thick dark hair, a small build, and refined movements. He seemed more New York than small-town North Carolina.

"He's brave to come out in public with all the hatred toward him," Colton said.

"Brave is one way to describe the man. Arrogant. Cocky. A little too sure of himself. Those are other ways to describe him." Cassidy rolled her eyes.

Colton's chuckle quickly faded. "I know what you're saying. Hopefully the situation will be resolved without too much heartache."

"Let's hope so." Cassidy glanced around. "But if you look at half of the people in here, they're giving Mr. Marks dirty looks right now."

Colton's gaze scanned the people around him and confirmed what Cassidy said was true. That guy might be the most hated person in the room right now. Before he could say anything else, the front door opened again. Someone new walked into the restaurant.

Someone Colton hadn't seen in a very long time.

The timing of him showing up here couldn't be a coincidence.

Colton stood and prepared himself to act.

CHAPTER FIFTEEN

"LEONARDO." Colton strode across the restaurant.

The man had short blond hair, a cleft chin, and carefully sculpted muscles. Put it all together, and he came across as someone who worked too hard to look tough. Something about Leonardo had never seemed authentic, and Colton had never forgotten that.

As Leonardo spotted Colton, the man's eyes widened with surprise and then . . . satisfaction.

"Colton . . ." The way he said the word showed the cockiness he was known for.

"What are you doing here?" Colton demanded.

Leonardo stepped back, some arrogance leaving his gaze. "I came to Lantern Beach looking for you."

Why in the world had he done that? Colton only knew he didn't want to have this conversation here—

there were too many people around. "You and I need to step outside."

Before the man could argue, Colton took Leonardo's arm and dragged him out the door to the small deck at the entrance.

"I don't know what's going on, man." Leonardo raised his hands in what looked like false innocence. "I just came here to talk."

Colton narrowed his gaze and shifted away from the glaring sun. He didn't want anything to stop him from seeing Leonardo's eyes and the truth—or lack thereof—there. "How did you find me?"

"I heard you'd started a new organization called Blackout. I wanted to see if I could get in on it."

Colton's jaw tightened. It sounded too easy. "Is that your story? And you just happened to show up today and come into the very restaurant where we are?"

Leonardo narrowed his eyes. "I don't know what's going on, man. But I'm telling the truth."

If he'd been trying to hide his presence, then he wouldn't have come into The Crazy Chefette. Leonardo was smarter than that. "When did you get into town?"

"Last night. Why?" Leonardo's hands went to his hips as his defenses seemed to go up.

"Did you come to the cottage last night?" Colton carefully watched Leonardo's expression. He was determined to get to the truth.

"What cottage?"

Colton felt his jaw tighten. "The cottage where Blackout meets."

"No, I got here just in time to check in at the inn. I didn't think this was going to be such a big deal. Sorry." He shrugged and let out a chuckle, making it clear he thought Colton was overreacting.

Colton wasn't ready to believe him yet, though. "You're saying you just happen to wander into this restaurant when we were here."

"It's like the only one on the island that's open. I thought it was fortuitous . . . but now I can see that it's obviously not." He scowled.

Colton took a step back, trying to get the best read on the situation. If Leonardo was telling the truth, his timing was awful. More than awful. It was horrendous.

"So, how do I get in on this new organization that you started?" All of Leonardo's defensiveness seemed to disappear, replaced by eagerness. This man had come here with a purpose and overly optimistic determination.

Colton shook his head, hating to burst his bubble. But he was going to have to.

Leonardo had been a SEAL, but he'd been kicked out because of insubordination. He was the last person Colton could see himself bringing on the team. When your life was on the line, you had to have people you could trust and depend on. Leonardo did not fit the bill.

"We're not hiring yet," Colton finally said.

"Can't you make an exception? I would be great for this job." His voice sounded unwavering with self-assurance.

"I'm not as confident of that fact as you are."

Leonardo's smile disappeared, and a dark cloud seemed to fill his gaze. "Look, just because I made one bad decision, that doesn't mean it should dictate the rest of my life."

"Unfortunately, in this line of work, that's sometimes what it does mean."

"You're saying you've never made a mistake?" Leonardo bristled, his stare burning into Colton's.

The night that Daniel died slammed into his mind. "No, I'm not saying that at all. But I always look out for my teammates."

Leonardo narrowed his gaze. "That's not what I heard."

Colton felt himself drawing his fist back. Before he did something he'd regret, someone grabbed his arm.

Ty appeared. His friend shook his head, a silent reminder that Colton needed to remain in control. He did. He couldn't let Leonardo get under his skin.

"If it isn't Ty Chambers," Leonardo continued with an almost bitter chuckle. "It's like a big party here, and I wasn't invited."

"Blackout is just getting off the ground," Ty said, his expression not softening. "I'm sorry you wasted your time by coming here."

Leonardo nodded, a cool look coming to his eyes. "I see how you are. Exclusive, just like always. I should've known better. Known that people don't change."

"You should have called first," Colton said, not buying into Leonardo's guilt trip.

"I wouldn't say it was for nothing. This place is beautiful." He glanced at the sand dunes in the distance. "In fact, maybe I'll stick around for a while."

Another surge of anger rushed through Colton. The last thing he wanted was for Leonardo to stay in Lantern Beach.

With one more dismissive shrug, Leonardo stepped back into The Crazy Chefette. Colton watched him through the glass door as he took a seat across the restaurant, a good distance away from Elise. He was thankful for that, at least.

"Do you think he was the guy outside the cottage last night?" Ty looked as tense as Colton felt as he turned toward him.

Colton remembered the figure. Remembered the man's stealth as he'd gotten away. "I find Leonardo's timing is suspicious."

"So do I. I've never trusted that guy, and his attempt to make us feel bad isn't going to change that."

"Same here. It looks like we have someone else to keep our eyes on."

"I agree. We do." This was just what he needed—something else to potentially distract him when Elise's life was in danger.

But the question remained in Colton's mind as to whether or not Leonardo had anything to do with the attack on Elise at her home.

Could he be the one who was working for the other side?

ELISE'S FOOD came while Colton was outside. She picked at her roast beef while watching the scene through the window beside her.

A few minutes later, the man Colton had confronted stomped back into the restaurant and slumped into a seat across the room. Where had Elise seen the man before? She felt certain that they'd met. Why had his conversation with Colton looked so heated?

"Do you think that guy's trouble?" Cassidy studied Elise's expression.

"At this point, I feel like anyone can be trouble." She set her fork down, her appetite waning.

Cassidy glanced back at the mystery man before

turning to Elise. "It looks like Colton and Ty took care of him."

Her words were true, but it didn't change the uneasy feeling in Elise's stomach.

A moment later, Colton and Ty strode back into the restaurant. Ty grabbed his drink before sliding into the booth next to Cassidy.

Colton remained quiet beside Elise. Instead of talking, he picked up a homemade potato chip and took a bite, a stormy look in his eyes.

Elise waited for the men to broach the subject. Thankfully, she wasn't disappointed.

"That was Leonardo," Colton started, his gaze still dark. "He heard we were here and he was hoping we would hire him."

"Leonardo Appleton?" Elise kept her voice low so as to not draw any attention.

"You remember him?" Colton asked.

"He looked familiar, but now that you said his name, I do. He really wanted a job?"

"That's right," Ty said.

"That takes a lot of guts." Cassidy raised her eyebrows. She'd stuck around to hear what was going on.

"Leonardo is gutsy, to say the least." Colton's gaze narrowed as he picked up another chip.

"Daniel said that he was kicked off the SEAL team," Elise said. "Is that correct?"

"He's one of the only guys I've ever known to actually be kicked off," Ty said. "I've seen other guys get demoted. But this man was just plain booted."

"I'm surprised to hear that," Cassidy said. "I figured that the vetting process for becoming a SEAL was so rigorous that all the bases were covered by the time they actually made it there."

"He started off as a great SEAL," Colton continued. "But, on one of his missions, a colleague died. He was shot and died in Leonardo's arms. Leonardo was never the same afterward and began acting erratically. At least, at first."

"Sounds like PTSD." Elise frowned.

"I suppose that was part of it." Colton glanced back at Leonardo and lowered his voice. "But his actions got to the point where the rest of his platoon couldn't rely on him or trust him. He blatantly disregarded orders on one mission. He was intoxicated, which is against the rules when you are on duty. His actions put his teammates' lives at risk. That, when coupled with other things, led him to get booted from the team."

"After all that, he really thinks you guys are going to want to hire him?" Cassidy asked.

"That's the other part of his problem," Ty said. "He's cocky and doesn't see the error of his ways."

Cassidy leaned closer. "You think he has anything to do with what's going on with Elise?"

Colton's jaw hardened. "I think that's the question we're all thinking about right now."

More unease sloshed inside Elise. When the person coming after her was faceless, it made everyone seem suspect. She prayed they'd get some answers soon so she could put this behind her.

They all ate for a few minutes in silence.

Cassidy's phone rang, and she put it to her ear. A moment later, she rose. "We have someone who is threatening to jump off the pier. He brought a gun as backup. I need to join Officer Dillinger and see if we can talk him down."

"Let me go with you." Elise stood also.

Cassidy froze and observed her. "I'm not sure that's a good idea."

"I'm not sure either." Colton wiped his mouth. "It's one thing to come to this restaurant where we can keep an eye on you in an enclosed space. It's another thing to go to the pier where you're out in the open."

"But I can help," Elise said. "Trauma is my specialty."

Cassidy glanced at Ty then Colton before looking back at Elise.

"You can come," Cassidy finally said. "I could use some backup, just in case my tactics don't work."

Elise nodded, grateful the chief was open to having her help. Finally, Elise felt like she could be of some use here. Though she didn't want to put herself in danger, situations like these were what she handled best.

She desperately needed to feel like she was doing something right.

CHAPTER SIXTEEN

COLTON DIDN'T like the thought of this. But Elise was her own person, and he didn't want to tell her what to do. Still, he was uneasy about how things might play out on the pier.

Elise would be exposed. If anyone wanted to take a shot at her, they'd have their chance. His muscles hardened at the thought.

He remained quiet and followed Cassidy's police cruiser to the scene. He pulled into the parking lot near the pier, noting one other police car was already there.

That still didn't make him feel better.

"You don't have to do this," Colton told Elise as he put his car in Park.

"I want to." Elise stared straight ahead, her gaze unwavering. "I want to help."

He opened his mouth to say more but then shut it again. There was no need to argue about this. Every minute mattered right now.

As they climbed from his car, Colton glanced around the mostly empty beach in the distance. He didn't see anything that screamed danger. But whoever these guys were, they were smarter than that, more subtle.

He put a hand on Elise's back as he led her up the steps and onto the pier. A small crowd had already gathered.

As they got closer, Colton spotted a man perched on the pier railing near the end of the 400-foot-long structure that jutted out over the water. The ocean below was not only deep but ice cold.

If the man went into the water and someone had to save him, the rescuer would also be putting his life on the line. The situation didn't look good.

Colton stayed close to Elise as they walked between those gathered. Mostly diehard fishermen were out here on this blustery day. Some hadn't even bothered to reel in their lines, but their fishing poles remained in holders on the edge of the pier, even as the fishermen's gazes focused on the scene in the distance.

A police line had been set up, and Braden stood guard. When he saw Colton and Elise, he pulled it up to let them through. He nodded at Elise, obviously recognizing her, but remained professional.

Colton and Elise stood in the background as Cassidy tried to talk to the man. The jumper appeared to be in his early forties. He had a fading hairline, evidence of severe acne, and, despite the cold weather, sweat covered his skin. As the man stared down into the ocean below, Colton saw the gun in one of his hands.

If he was going to jump from the pier, why had he also brought a gun? Was it in case he changed his mind about the method of death? Colton supposed that it didn't matter, but it just seemed odd.

Cassidy stood a few feet away, her body language looking surprisingly relaxed. Colton knew that was probably purposeful. She was trying to put the guy at ease.

"I'm the police chief here. My name is Cassidy. What's yours?"

"Henry. I've done enough talking." The man's voice trembled as he stared at Cassidy. "I don't want to do this anymore."

"You don't want to do what, Henry?" Cassidy's voice sounded calm and even.

"I don't want to live. You are not going to change my mind. Just leave me alone. I didn't want anyone to see me."

"We can't leave you alone."

His nostrils flared, as if her response annoyed him.

"I didn't ask any of you to come here. I figured no one would be paying attention."

"Why don't you at least give me the gun?" Cassidy reached an arm out. As she did, the wind tugged her hair from its neat bun. The weather was bitterly cold out here with nothing to block the wind.

"I can't." Henry raised his weapon. "I need it."

Everyone nearby seemed to duck as the barrel swung around.

"Let's not point that thing at anyone," Cassidy said, tension stringing through her voice. "Why do you need it?"

Henry lowered the gun back to the weathered wooden railing, but his finger remained on the trigger. "You wouldn't understand."

"Try me."

He squeezed his eyes shut and shook his head with more force than necessary. "It's not supposed to be like this."

"How is it supposed to be then?" Cassidy stepped closer, her actions purposeful and calm.

"Alice was never supposed to leave me." His voice cracked again, and his face started to contort into a frown.

"Who is Alice?" Cassidy asked.

"My wife." The man glanced below. As he shifted, the action caused him to sway backward, teetering on the railing.

The crowds gasped as Henry nearly lost his balance and toppled into the ocean. He caught himself just in time. The man's face looked even more tense as he glanced at Cassidy.

Something in his gaze seemed to scream for help, to speak desperation. He didn't really want to do this, did he?

"Where is Alice now?" Cassidy continued.

"I don't know. She left me. I came here hoping to start over. But now I realize I don't want to go on without her." Sobs escaped between his words.

Colton glanced behind him at the crowd, looking for any more signs of trouble. A familiar face appeared. The homeless man that they'd run into last night—Jason, if he remembered correctly. He'd joined the fishermen and everyone else who gazed at the scene before them.

But Jason's gaze appeared to be on Elise.

Colton's muscles tightened. What if there was more to this man than he was letting on? He'd only shown up here three days ago. If the wrong person had caught wind that certain information had been discovered, they may have sent someone here to keep an eye on the former SEAL team.

As the homeless man wove through the crowd closer to the police tape, Colton braced himself to act.

ELISE PULLED her gaze away from the man on the pier long enough to glance at Colton. But Colton wasn't paying attention to what was going on right now. His gaze was focused on someone else instead—the homeless man they'd run into last night.

What was Jason doing here? Had he come to start trouble? Or was the man just loitering on the pier to pass time?

Elise turned her gaze away from him in time to hear Henry say, "Life isn't worth it anymore."

He started to stand—on the railing.

"You don't want to do that," Cassidy said.

"I don't know what I want," he said. "I guess I need to get help. Serious help. I just wish there was someone who understood..."

Cassidy glanced at Elise and nodded. That was her invitation to step in. The situation had escalated.

Elise wiped her hands on her jeans and paced closer. "Henry, my name is Elise. I want to help you."

"It's too late for that." The man managed to stand, gun still in hand, and he wobbled as he tried to find his balance. "I don't want to go on anymore."

"I don't think you're telling yourself the truth."

He glanced at her, his eyes narrowed, as if Elise's words surprised him. "What do you mean?"

"I mean that if you had wanted to jump, you would have already. There's a part of you deep down inside that wants someone to talk you out of this. That wants someone else to help, to let you know there's still hope."

"I don't know what you're talking about." He shook his head rapidly and stared down at the water below.

Elise stepped closer. "I lost my husband too, you know."

He glanced back at her again, something registering in his eyes. "Is that right?"

"It is." Her head spun as she looked at the vast nothingness behind the man. Spray from the waves occasionally reached them, and the water felt icy. A strong wind made the situation even worse.

"When did he leave you?" Henry asked.

"It was worse than that. We were going to separate. Before we could, he died."

Henry's gaze latched onto hers for a moment. "I'm sorry to hear that. But that doesn't change what I need to do. I don't want to live like this anymore."

"I know you're going through some dark days, but I'm here to let you know that it's going to get better." Elise meant the words. Even with what she was going through now, hope pushed her onward.

"That's what people say. But I feel like I've been living in this darkness for too long."

"That's how it's going to feel for a while," Elise said. "But we can get help. It's not going to happen overnight, but it *can* happen."

"I've given up hope that I can be helped." His lips pulled down, as if fighting back a sob.

"That's because you're not thinking straight right now. You're letting your heart and your grief do all the talking and decision-making in your life. Don't let your emotions win. There are other parts of you that are stronger than this. If you quiet yourself for a minute and silence the other voices, you can hear the part of you that still believes in hope."

The man didn't say anything for a moment.

Colton touched Elise's arm, but she didn't turn to him. She didn't want to break this moment. She was close to making a breakthrough.

"Henry, you have value," she continued.

"I used to love life." A sob escaped the man. "The future seemed so bright."

"It can seem bright again."

He turned and his eyes met hers. "Do you mean it?"

"I do. Will you give the police your gun? I'm afraid somebody else may get hurt."

He remained silent for another moment. Finally, he raised his gun. Barrel out.

Pointed at Elise.

She held her breath as she waited to see what would happen next.

CHAPTER SEVENTEEN

COLTON TENSED as he watched Henry turn and raise his gun. Colton's muscles poised for action, ready to tackle Elise if he needed to. Whatever it took to protect her.

What was the man thinking? Was he going to pull the trigger? On Elise?

"Take your finger off the trigger." Cassidy stepped forward, pushing Elise back some.

Colton held his breath, waiting to see what the man would do.

Henry looked at his gun. Looked at Elise. Finally, the man lowered his arm and handed his weapon to Cassidy.

Colton released his breath.

Thank God. Things could have turned out so much differently.

There was still so much that could go wrong here.

As a freezing wind blew over the pier, Colton looked back at the crowd again, scanning them for any signs of trouble as he listened to Elise continue to coach the man. She definitely had a way with people. But that was something Colton would have to admire later, when they were someplace safe.

His gaze went to Jason again. He watched as the man glanced over at someone else.

Colton's gaze followed his. Another man had joined them at the pier. The new guy didn't fit in with the rest of the crowd. He was dressed too nicely, looking more like he should be at a business meeting than at the beach.

That said, something about the man reminded Colton of a shark. Maybe it was the tuft of light brown hair that the man had styled in somewhat of a mohawk on top of his head. Maybe it was the matching goatee that was long and pointed.

Colton's muscles tightened as he saw the two exchange looks and mutter something to each other. What was that about?

Colton looked back at Elise. She spoke in low tones to Henry. Colton felt certain the man was on the verge of getting down from the railing.

"Let us help you," Elise continued, pulling her sweater closer as the wind continued to freeze everything in its path.

"I want help." The man's voice quivered. He crouched now, as if he might get down.

"Then take it."

Henry froze for a minute and then nodded.

The man started to turn. Just as he did, a bang sounded in the distance.

Duck hunters, Colton assumed. The sound echoed all over the island during this season.

Colton's gaze swerved back to the jumper. Henry's eyes widened.

The next instant, his arms flailed as he began to slip.

Cassidy lunged toward him.

Before she could catch him, he plummeted from the pier.

Colton's stomach clenched as he rushed toward the railing.

"The Coast Guard is still ten minutes out," Cassidy said.

"I can get him. I was always the top swimmer in BUD/S." Colton paused for only a second to kick off his shoes. "Keep an eye on Elise."

Before anybody could stop him, Colton climbed the railing and dove into the water.

Icy tentacles burrowed into his skin. The sheer frigidness of the water took his breath away as his body was submerged in the frosty depths of the ocean.

He pushed himself to the surface and sucked a

deep breath of cold air. He glanced around, looking for Henry.

The man was nowhere to be seen.

Taking another deep breath, Colton dove back beneath the surface. The water was too murky to see much, but he had no choice. He knew in these conditions, the man didn't have long. No one could survive out here for an extended period of time.

Colton stayed under for as long as he could before breaking the surface again. He glanced around, hoping to catch a glimpse of Henry. His limbs were already starting to feel numb, and the waves were pulling him out farther into the ocean.

He knew the truth about being in water this cold. His surface blood vessels were constricting as his body tried to protect vital organs. His blood pressure and heart rate were increasing. The first thing he would lose were his motor skills.

The average person had fifteen minutes until they lost consciousness.

Colton had to find the man. Soon.

Or they would both be goners.

ELISE GRIPPED THE RAILING, her lungs tight. She squeezed her eyes shut and lifted up a prayer for both Colton and Henry.

They had been so close to everything turning out okay. Then someone had to fire that gun. The timing couldn't have been worse.

She felt a hand on her shoulder and turned to see Cassidy. The chief put her phone back into her pocket. "I just called for backup. Ty's on his way to the beach right now to assist also."

"I'm afraid neither of them will survive those conditions out there." She stared down at tumultuous water and felt her head spin.

"Colton was a SEAL. If anybody can do this, he can."

Elise forced herself to nod, though numbness started to spread through her. The outlook seemed bleak and the task impossible.

"We need to get down to the beach," Cassidy said. "I can't leave you here alone. Come with me. Braden, you too. Keep an eye out for trouble."

They followed Cassidy as she strode through the crowd.

Maybe they shouldn't have come out here. If Elise hadn't insisted then Colton's life wouldn't be on the line right now. She pushed away the self-reprimand, knowing it would get her nowhere. She'd have to address it later.

As she hurried behind Cassidy, Elise glanced back down into the tumultuous ocean. Colton popped back up out of the water. By himself.

Nausea rumbled inside her.

He still hadn't found Henry. Knowing Colton, he wouldn't leave until he did.

On the one hand, Elise admired his tenacity. On the other hand, she feared for his safety. He'd always been a protector.

But who would protect him?

At the end of the pier, they hurried down the steps and rushed onto the sand. Another sharp gust of wind coming off the water hit them. If it was that cold on land, she could only imagine how cold it was in the water.

Please, Lord. Protect them. Keep them safe.

"Paramedics are on their way," Cassidy said as they paused by the shore.

Ty sprinted from a shack in the distance, a flotation device in his hands. He must have just gotten here in time to see what happened. "I'm going out there. Colton is going to need some help getting in, and we don't have time to wait."

"Be careful." Cassidy touched his forearm a moment too long. Elise knew the woman didn't want to let her husband go.

Elise had lived that feeling more times than she could count.

"I will." Without saying anything else, Ty dove into the water and began swimming toward Colton.

Elise pressed her eyes closed.

No more losses, Elise told herself. Her heart couldn't take many more. She'd already lost Daniel. She couldn't handle the thought of losing Colton also. Now Ty had also been thrown into the mix.

When she opened her eyes, her gaze went to Cassidy. Though the woman remained professional, the tension on her face was obvious. She was worried as well. Cassidy's eyes remained fixed on the scene in the distance.

Elise pulled her arms over her chest, fighting off the cold. The water lapped at their shoes as they stood on the shore. The ocean—a thing of such beauty—could also be so dangerous.

A Bible verse from Isaiah that Daniel had kept on his desk slammed into Elise's mind. *When you pass through the waters, I will be with you; and when you pass through the rivers, they will not sweep over you.*

Be with them, she prayed. *Please. Don't let these waters sweep them away.*

Just then, an eerie feeling washed over Elise. She froze and turned. Was someone watching her? Was that why her senses were on alert?

The hair on her neck rose. Suddenly she felt more exposed than ever. From here, anyone on the pier would have sight of her. There was also a row of houses behind her, and several people had gathered on the beach in the distance—plenty of places for the bad guy to lurk, to wait for the right opportunity to enact his plan.

Someone still wanted her dead . . . right after they got the information from her. She couldn't forget that.

As if reading her thoughts, Braden squeezed in closer. She appreciated the fact that people were watching out for her. But mostly she just wanted Colton, Ty, and Henry to be okay.

CHAPTER EIGHTEEN

COLTON KNEW he didn't have much time. If he couldn't find Henry soon, he was going to have to make a hard choice.

Just as the thought entered his head, he saw a hand flailing through the water.

Henry.

That had to be him.

Colton swam against the current, determined to rescue the man. Just as he reached the spot, the hand disappeared under the water again.

Using his last bit of strength, Colton dove beneath the waves. He reached for the figure tossing back and forth and wrapped an arm across the man's chest.

It was Henry.

The man was barely conscious, but he was alive. Colton felt a faint heartbeat.

Surfacing, Colton began the swim back to shore. He paced himself, his muscles straining as he fought the ocean. He had no choice but to push forward. It was just a matter of time before hypothermia kicked in. He couldn't let that happen.

Every time he closed his eyes, all he could think about was Elise. Colton needed to be there for her. If something happened to him, who would keep an eye on her? Who would clear Daniel's name?

He glanced at the pier again. Though his gaze was blurry with saltwater, he saw the people staring at him from above. Blinking, he spotted the homeless man still standing there, still watching. The other man who'd been with him was now gone. At least, Colton couldn't see him.

He needed to find out what his story was. Right now, everyone was a suspect.

He looked forward. Had Colton even made any progress? Was he closer to the shore or was that just an illusion?

Colton had been in far worse situations as a SEAL. But he'd always had his team to back him up. If there was one thing the military had taught him, it was the importance of not thinking you could do things alone.

A flashback hit him of the night Daniel died.

They'd been on that boat. In the middle of the night. With no light around, it was nearly impossible to see anything.

He'd looked up in time to see Daniel running toward one of the Savages. That's when someone else had appeared on the top deck, his gun aimed.

Before Colton could stop the guy, the man had fired.

The bullet hit Daniel.

His friend fell into the water.

Colton had dived in after him . . . but Daniel was gone. His body was nowhere to be found.

To this day, it still hadn't been recovered.

His team had gone back several times after the mission to look for him again.

They'd had no success.

Colton squelched those memories—for now. He had to focus. Regret would only slow him down.

Colton felt his breathing becoming shallower. Too shallow. The cold water was taking a toll on him, zapping his energy and freezing his muscles.

He fought to remain in control. Keeping himself in the right mental space was half the battle. *You can do this, Colton. Just keep moving.*

As he glanced up again, he saw the homeless man still peering at him from above. Colton knew what that meant.

He was barely moving here in this water, making no real progress.

The waves and rip current kept pushing him out,

and Colton had spent too much energy searching for Henry.

He needed a backup plan, and he needed it now. Colton wasn't going to get out on his own.

Just as the thought entered his head, he heard a faint voice in the distance.

"Colton!"

He turned just in time to see Ty cut through the water, a bright orange floatation device with him.

Relief flashed through Colton. He should've known his friend would be there for him. Between the two of them, maybe they could all get back to land.

ELISE COULDN'T PULL her gaze away from the water where the rescue took place. She held her breath, waiting, praying.

"Ty reached them," Cassidy said.

Some of Elise's anxiety faded as she realized Cassidy was right. Ty and Colton were the most experienced guys a person could have out there. They were going to be okay.

A shout sounded behind her, and she turned. Dez and Griff rushed from the parking lot toward the scene.

"We just heard what happened." Dez paused in

front of them, his gaze searching the water. "What's the update?"

"They found the man who jumped, and now Ty and Colton are trying to get him to shore," Cassidy said. "But the rip currents are bad today, and the water is frigid."

"Is there a boat on the way?" Dez asked.

"I called for one, but it's still five minutes out."

"They don't have five minutes." Griff frowned. "The best thing to do in a situation like this is to float. But he'll never get to shore doing that."

As he said the words, a siren sounded in the distance. Good news. Paramedics were almost here. All three of the men would need to be treated as soon as they got to the shore.

Dez glanced around, his eyes steely hard with determination. "Are there any more flotation devices?"

"In the lifeguard shack behind us," Cassidy said. "It's where all the rescue equipment is kept. Ty unlocked it."

Dez took off toward the building, Griff right behind him. They appeared a few minutes later with flotation devices in hand. Before anyone could talk them out of it, both men dove into the water.

Ty and Colton were now closer to the shoreline. But they were still far enough away to be in danger.

Elise held her breath and waited to see what would happen.

"They've got this," Braden said beside her.

She knew that they did. But until they were all on dry land, she wouldn't be able to relax.

Finally, the men were close enough that she could see their heads bobbing. She could make out the features of their faces.

They were almost here.

Please, Lord.

A few minutes later, they rose from the water. They stood beside each other. Their arms linked together as they fought the current and tried to walk the rest of the way.

The breath left Elise's lungs.

They were really okay.

Elise took a step toward Colton. But, before she could reach him, paramedics surrounded the men.

Elise froze, letting them do their jobs.

She'd have time to talk to Colton later, to tell him how worried she'd been.

She wished she could say the danger was over, but she knew the truth was far from it.

CHAPTER NINETEEN

COLTON TRIED NOT to be impatient as the paramedic took his vitals in the back of the ambulance in the pier parking lot. Two other ambulances were also on scene treating his friends and Henry.

He knew his friends were okay—he wasn't sure about Henry, though. At least the man still had a heartbeat when they'd come ashore. That was one thing to be thankful about.

Braden had brought them dry clothes, and Colton had been able to change in the back of the ambulance. He already felt warmer being out of the soaking wet clothing.

As the paramedic checked his heart rate again, Colton glanced over the man's shoulder. He spotted Elise standing with Cassidy. Her arms were crossed, and a pensive expression captured her features.

She'd been worried about him, he realized.

Colton was thankful the situation had turned out as it did. But there were too many people around for his comfort right now. Any one of these people in the crowd could be the person who had tried to kill Elise.

The paramedic cleared him, and Colton stood. "How's Henry?"

"We're taking him to the clinic for further observation, but he should be fine."

Colton glanced over at the man as he lay on a stretcher inside the ambulance. An oxygen mask covered his face, an IV had been hooked up, and multiple blankets covered him.

Henry was alive. That was a good thing.

With a final nod, Colton stepped toward Elise. That seemed to be all the invitation she needed. She crossed to him in five strides and wrapped her arms around his neck.

"I'm so glad you're okay," she murmured.

Just the feel of Elise against him made Colton feel things he shouldn't. Yet he couldn't push her away. The selfish part of him loved every minute of attention this woman gave him.

"Everything worked out," he said.

She stepped back, her wide eyes still on him. "You had me pretty worried. That was awfully brave of you to go in after that man."

"Well, you convinced me that he had a brighter

future than he even realized. It would be a shame if you didn't have a chance to prove that true."

A small smile fluttered across her lips. "You're a good man, Colton Locke."

Hearing her say those words caused something warm to spread inside him. Having her admiration was a great gift. But what would she think if she learned the truth? The fleeing warmth was replaced by a cold more painful than the ocean water in winter.

"We need to get you back to the cottage now." Colton scanned the crowd around him again. "I don't like you being out here."

"I'm ready to get back myself." She shivered.

With one final glance behind him, he led Elise back to his car.

He was so thankful that everything had turned out well. But the images that battered him from that last mission with Daniel had left their bruises again. Or was it that the bruises had never healed in the first place?

Colton didn't know. But he felt beat up—both physically and emotionally.

Those wounds were ones he wasn't sure he'd ever recover from.

BACK AT THE HOUSE, Colton went to his cabana

and took a long, hot shower. While he did that, Elise warmed up their lunch. Someone had packaged the food from the restaurant and dropped it by the house. The gesture had been kind.

Griff and Dez were at their cabanas working on a few things, and Ty and Cassidy had gone to dinner with some friends.

Elise felt grateful she'd have a moment alone with Colton. The thought was crazy and unexpected. But seeing him almost die today—at least, in her mind, that's what could have happened—had caused something to shift inside her.

She wasn't sure what that was or what it meant. She only knew that Colton was entirely more important to her than she'd ever realized.

Though it seemed like it had only been an hour since they'd had lunch, in actuality, the whole ordeal at the pier had taken several hours. The sun was beginning to set, and the day to wind down.

Her breath caught when she saw Colton step back into the house. His hair still glistened with water. He wore jeans and a long-sleeved blue shirt that fit just right.

But it was his eyes that captured her attention. How had Elise never noticed how beautiful they were?

She cleared her throat. "I heated up our lunch."

"Perfect." He cast her a quick smile. "How about if

we grab the food and sit on the couch to eat? Too informal?"

"No, that sounds perfect." She picked up her plate and some seltzer water and sat cross-legged on the couch.

But her thoughts were heavy. She'd wondered for a moment that she was going to lose Colton . . . just like she'd lost Daniel. That possibility caused something to shatter inside her.

"Are you okay, Elise?"

Colton's soft voice pulled her from her trancelike state. She wanted to nod, to say yes. But she couldn't. She set her plate beside his on the coffee table.

"I was afraid . . . you were going to die." She pressed her eyes closed as she heard the vulnerability in her voice. "I can't lose Daniel and you too."

"Oh, Elise . . ." Colton reached for her and pulled her close.

She didn't argue when he tucked an arm around her and her head pressed against his chest. The steady rhythm of his heartbeat brought her a strong comfort.

She almost wished he never had to let her go.

But that thought was crazy.

Colton was like a big brother.

Reluctantly, she pulled back and tried to compose herself. "I'm sorry."

"Don't apologize."

The look in Colton's eyes . . . the sound of his voice . . . nearly melted her with its tenderness.

She had to get herself together before she caved in to all her emotions and did something she regretted. Instead, she scooted back and took a bite of her warm roast beef. The meal definitely hit the spot, as did the savory scent of beef that floated up to her.

"Do you remember the first time we ever met?" Elise took a long sip of her water and watched Colton's expression. Based on the look in his eyes, he clearly did remember that day.

"How could I forget?"

Colton had stopped by to pick something up for Daniel. Elise had answered. She'd been surprised by the beefy, giant man who stood there. She'd assumed Colton was the plumber she'd called, and she ushered him inside to show him the leak in her bathroom.

She'd thought it was weird he had no tools to do the job, but she'd been desperate and hadn't asked any questions. Daniel had been working overseas for the past four months, and it seemed like everything in the house was falling apart.

"You thought I was the plumber." Colton shook his head.

"In my defense, I didn't get your message before you came."

He chuckled.

It had become a running joke between them after

that. Every time he'd come over, he'd ask how the pipes in the house were working.

It hadn't always been happy times, though. That SEAL team had gone through a lot together. Too much, it seemed sometimes.

At the thought, Elise reached forward. At the edge of his sleeve, Elise could see the scars that had turned Colton's life upside down. She ran a finger beneath them, her thoughts turning heavy.

"Does that day still give you grief?"

"I still feel the scars. The skin is tighter."

She dropped her hand and frowned. Memories pummeled her—memories of the phone call from Daniel about what had happened.

"I still remember the day I got the news that you had been injured by an IED," she said, her throat tight. "I remember fearing the worst."

Colton rubbed his arm. "It seemed like it could go either way for a while there. I'm thankful that I just came out with a few scars. I would have been dead if it weren't for Daniel."

"He never said it that way."

Colton shook his head. "Of course he didn't. But he seemed to sense there were IEDs in the area where I was. He called to me just as I heard the pressure plate click. I was able to throw myself out of the way. I'm lucky to be alive."

Something dark crossed his gaze. Elise assumed it

was because of the memories of that day. But why did there seem to be a touch of grief there also?

"I am sorry about what happened with Vicki afterward," she said quietly. She rested her hand on his forearm, desperate to offer comfort. "She was a fool to break up with you."

Colton shrugged. As quickly as his dark mood appeared, it disappeared. "At the time, I felt like it was a horrible thing to happen. But I realized that I didn't really love her. We enjoyed spending time together when I was here, but, looking back, there really wasn't much substance, you know?"

"I guess it's better that you discovered that before you took the relationship any further."

A soft smile feathered his lips. "Yeah, I guess you're right."

As Elise looked up at him, she realized that, in her mind, Daniel's face had somehow morphed into Colton's. It made no sense. How had this man edged his way into her heart so quickly?

Guilt squeezed at her. That hadn't been what she had intended. She wasn't supposed to like Colton or to get close. That would only end in trouble. Being attracted to Colton felt like a betrayal to Daniel.

And Elise already felt like she'd failed her husband, especially considering their last conversation before he died.

CHAPTER TWENTY

COLTON WAS KEENLY aware of how warm and cozy Elise looked as she sat beside him. He was aware of Elise's hand on his arm. Of how their legs brushed.

He wasn't complaining.

Certainly, she didn't do this with her patients, did she?

The simple touch brought such an immense comfort that he never wanted her to move.

As hard as today had been, this moment right now made it all worth it. This brief time where Colton had been reminded that he wasn't alone in this world or alone in his grief. Elise understood. As much as he wanted to take that hurt from her, he couldn't. But they could have this moment.

As he looked over at her, his heart pounded in his ears.

From the very first moment Colton had met the woman, he'd been blown away. Maybe he'd never gotten married because he'd been waiting for his very own Elise. The problem was that no other woman measured up.

He'd always admired her. She'd been Daniel's equal. She was strong, smart, tough—but also soft and kind. The perfect blend.

As Colton stared at Elise now, he opened his mouth, though he wasn't sure what words were about to emerge. Before he could say anything, the door opened.

Elise pulled her hand back and straightened.

Colton watched as the gang flooded inside.

He'd asked them to meet, hadn't he?

How he wished he hadn't.

"This still a good time?" Dez asked, something glimmering in his gaze.

Colton stood. "Yes, absolutely. Have a seat."

"I'll get these dishes cleaned up, and I'll get out of your way." Elise grabbed their leftover food and carried it back into the kitchen.

"Why don't you stay?"

Elise froze and slowly turned to look at him. "Really?"

"Really. This is your life we're talking about. You should be in the loop."

After a moment, she nodded. "I won't argue."

"SO WHAT DO we have so far?" Colton started as they all sat in the living room ready to debrief.

He had his computer as well as a pad of paper in front of him and had gone into leader mode. Gone was the soft side of him she'd seen earlier—the side that was achingly tender and concerned with her. She flushed every time she thought about it.

Elise had never been in on the action before, and it felt weird to be here. Yet she was grateful for the opportunity. She had the most at stake here.

"I'll start," Colton said. "Benjamin is talking to Tara Campbell's boyfriend. He should be back tomorrow evening, so hopefully he'll have an update for us. In the meantime, I've been examining those pictures that were left, but I haven't gotten very far. I've made a list of everyone I recognize in the photos. The normal players are there. The commander. Secretary Stabler. I'm still not sure where these photos were taken, though, or why these are important."

Dez raised his hand. "I'll go next. I sent the code to my friend Kari. I didn't tell her where we found it or any of the details. She promised discretion and said she would get right on it. I'm hoping to hear something from her anytime."

"Good news," Colton said.

"I've been looking into the number Daniel called

from the burner phone," Griff said. "The calls went to another burner. I was able to ascertain, thanks to a friend of mine, that the device was activated while in the DC area."

"Some news is better than no news," Colton said. "But we need to make more progress."

Elise's throat tightened. She knew his words were true. Time wasn't on their side, though.

Someone was willing to kill to get that information. But what else could they do?

She had no idea.

CHAPTER TWENTY-ONE

COLTON COULDN'T GET Elise out of his mind. It didn't make sense. He and Elise could never be together for so many reasons. Not only was she his best friend's girl, but if she knew the truth about what happened that night, everything would change.

He would be wise to keep that in mind.

He went back to his cabana, ready to settle in for the evening. But first he had some research of his own that he wanted to do. Today's events had put him back. He intended on spending most of the day researching that information Elise had found.

He stood and paced over to the window again. As he shoved the curtain aside, he saw movement by the sand dune. His muscles tensed. Grabbing his gun, he stepped outside.

This guy wasn't going to get away again. Not on his watch.

COLTON REMAINED in the shadows as he moved toward the dark figure in the distance. Who was this person? Was this the same man who'd tried to kill Elise?

He didn't know, but he was going to find out.

Colton remained low, watching his every step so as not to give away his location. But he knew the reality was that whoever was out there had already seen him. This person had probably been watching this whole place, just waiting for the sun to go down so he could make his next move.

Whoever was out there hadn't moved. Colton could clearly see the man still crouching by the sand dune. What was this man planning?

Colton decided to go around the side of Ty's cottage and come up on the other side of the sand dune. He hoped the tactical move might throw his watcher off.

He cut underneath Ty's house and crossed the dune. Still careful to stay low and to let the darkness conceal him, Colton reached the figure and raised his gun.

"Who are you? And what are you doing here?"

Colton blinked rapidly as the man stepped closer, and Benjamin's features came into view.

"Benjamin?"

He raised his hands in the air. "Wow. What's going on? I'm just sitting here watching the ocean."

Now that Colton thought about it, the man hadn't been crouching. He'd been sitting. But from a distance, it had been hard to tell the difference.

"You weren't supposed to be back until tomorrow." Colton tucked his gun into his waistband, irritation still rippling his muscles.

"The job ended early," Benjamin said. "Alayna went back home to DC and cut her trip short."

"Why wasn't I informed of the change?"

"It was spontaneous. She told me today at five and then she left. So I came back."

"And you didn't call?"

"I didn't think it was a big deal." Benjamin shrugged, his shoulders looking stiff with defensiveness. "I didn't know it was a crime to come back when the job was done or to sit outside and watch the ocean."

"We've had a lot going on, and we're all on edge right now."

Benjamin remained quiet a moment, as if mentally shaking off his prickliness in favor of curiosity. "What's happening?"

Colton paused, contemplating how much to say. He

wanted to trust Benjamin. Wanted to think of the man as a little brother. But there were still questions Colton had that Benjamin hadn't answered to his satisfaction. The fact that Benjamin had returned early without telling anybody also raised red flags. What was the real reason he hadn't called or announced his arrival?

Colton had to remain cautious, not only for his own safety, but for the safety of everyone around him.

"You're telling me you got back a couple hours ago?" Colton clarified.

Benjamin's gaze remained cool. "Yeah, that's right."

"And if I check the ferry records, I'll see if that's true? I can confirm that a car with your license plate was on it at approximately that time?"

"Look, what's with the third degree? Don't you trust me?" Benjamin raised his hands, as if giving up.

"I didn't say that."

"Do people think I'm involved in some way with this current situation?"

"I didn't say that either."

Benjamin shook his head. "You didn't deny it either."

"Look, Ben—"

Benjamin snorted and stepped back. "Do you know what? Never mind. I'm tired, and I think I'm going to turn in early tonight."

Colton considered calling him back so they could

finish the conversation. But Colton realized he had nothing else to say. Not right now.

First, he needed to figure out his next move.

And he needed to figure out if he trusted all his men.

CHAPTER TWENTY-TWO

CASSIDY AND TY both woke up early the next morning. Though Cassidy loved having everybody at her house, it was nice to have a few minutes alone with Ty. Especially with everything that had been going on so far this week.

Ty fixed her some coffee along with a bagel spread with blueberry cream cheese. Though today was cold and blustery outside, they both bundled up and stepped onto the screened porch. Being out here was one of their favorite things to do together, especially to watch the sunrise over the Atlantic Ocean as they began their day. Kujo sat at their feet as they sat on the swing, gliding back and forth.

"It's been a crazy couple days, huh?" Ty said.

"You can say that again. Things are never calm

around here, though." To think Cassidy had assumed being police chief on a small island would be easy...

"What are the updates with the hotel development?"

She lowered her coffee mug. "The surveyor is supposed to come today. There are numerous steps that need to take place first, but some of the community groups are threatening lawsuits. If this hotel does get built, it's going to take a long time for them to jump through all these legal loopholes."

"I feel like this is taking a toll on you." Ty rested his hand on her back as he studied her face.

Cassidy shrugged. "I can't say it's not taking a toll on me. I just hate to see people here so divided. That was the one thing that we always did right here on the island. We stayed together."

Ty frowned and nodded. His arm stretched across the back of the swing. "Hopefully, this will pass. I suppose that having all these people from my past here only adds to the craziness."

"Do you regret it?"

"No, not at all. These people are like my family."

She had a feeling he'd say that. She'd expected nothing less. "So what about Colton and Elise?"

He glanced at her in surprise. "What about them?"

"Is it just me, or is there something there between them? I saw the way they were looking at each other yesterday. They seemed pretty cozy and comfortable."

Ty shrugged. "I think they would be good together, but there's a lot they need to overcome if that's going to ever happen."

She nodded, letting the swing continue to sway back and forth. "Do you think they're both ready to move on after losing Daniel?"

"Knowing both of them . . . I would say yes. They're both mature, and they don't use their emotions as a crutch. I could see it working."

"Why do I feel like there's a but in there?"

Ty let out a long breath. "Something happened when Daniel died. I don't know what it was, and I know it's not my business. But I know there's more to the story. They said they were doing a training exercise out there. But I don't know why they would be doing training exercises out in that area of the Mediterranean Sea. I've never heard of anything like that before."

"So if it wasn't a training exercise, then what was it?" Cassidy licked some cream cheese from her finger.

Ty gave her a look and shrugged. "Things that aren't supposed to be mentioned."

"You mean like an off-the-book operation?"

"Exactly."

"And something like that could have the potential to tear them apart before they even start, can't it?" She frowned. She'd had happy visions of the two of them falling in love. She was so happy with Ty that she wanted everyone to be happy.

"Unfortunately, I would say yes."

Cassidy took a sip of her coffee as she contemplated that. It wasn't her business, nor was it her concern. But she was curious to see how this would play out, and she hoped it worked out for the best for everyone.

She set her bagel on a little table beside her and shifted toward Ty. "There's one other thing I think you should know. I was going to tell you last night, but I was too exhausted to get into it."

"What is it?"

She frowned, wishing her words weren't the truth. "After the town meeting . . . somebody pulled me aside. They have concerns about Blackout being located here in Lantern Beach."

A knot formed between his eyebrows. "Why in the world would anyone have a concern about that?"

"This person thinks that the organization might bring more danger to the otherwise peaceful island."

"What danger have we brought?" His voice rose with emotion. "Most of our missions have been off this island. This is just a meeting place."

"I guess this guy got mad at Colton during the protest, and now he's trying to make life difficult."

"Who is this guy?"

"Ron Davis."

Ty blinked. "Ron is giving you a hard time? I didn't see him as the type."

"I guess these situations can bring out the worst in people."

"I guess so."

Cassidy nudged Ty's chin up. "Hey, it's not all bad news."

"Give me some good news then."

"Look at that sunrise." She nodded toward the ocean, where brilliant bursts of yellow, coral, and purple exploded in the sky. "The way the clouds are formed today almost makes it look like the hand of God is right there holding the sun in the sky for us."

Ty let out a breath. "You're right. It's a good reminder."

"I have those every once in a while."

He cast a smile at her before planting a quick kiss on her lips. "Yes, you do."

CHAPTER TWENTY-THREE

WHEN ELISE WOKE up the next morning, she found a note from Cassidy on the kitchen table saying that she had already gone into work, but that Elise could help herself to the bagels and coffee that had been left out. Ty was outside working on his truck and keeping an eye on the place.

Sitting down, she petted Kujo on the head. "At least I've got you, right?"

She'd just settled at the kitchen table with her coffee and bagel when the door opened. Her breath caught as she anticipated seeing Colton.

Instead, Benjamin James stood there. He looked the same as ever with his baby face, short dark hair, and broad build. Daniel had always teased him, calling him Angel Eyes.

Those very angelic eyes widened, mirroring Elise's

surprise.

"Elise . . . you're here."

She stood and pulled him into a hug. "Benjamin. You haven't changed at all since I saw you last."

He stepped back, his hands still grasping her arms. "And you look great too, Ms. Oliver."

Elise tilted her head in mock offense. "Ms. Oliver? Now you're making me feel old."

She was only eight years older than Benjamin, but Daniel had almost been like a father figure to him. Daniel had always thought Benjamin had potential to be one of the best SEALs out there. Yet she also sensed a disconnect between Benjamin and the rest of the guys.

She didn't ask and figured it wasn't her business.

Benjamin grinned and dropped his arms. "Okay, Elise it is then. It's great to see you here."

"Why don't you sit down? I'll fix you some coffee."

He didn't argue. A few minutes later, they were seated across from each other and catching up on old times.

Toward the end of the conversation, Benjamin's eyes narrowed. "I wish different circumstances had brought you here."

"Me too." She sighed. "Believe me, me too."

"It sounds like I missed a lot while I was gone."

COLTON FROZE when he walked into the room and saw Benjamin and Elise chatting away at the kitchen table like old friends. Part of him wanted to warn Elise that Benjamin may not be trustworthy. But Colton knew he couldn't say those words aloud.

Instead, he felt his jaw stiffen as he went over to the table to say hello to each of them.

Seeing Elise's eyes light up when she saw him caused Colton's heartbeat to accelerate.

"Good morning." She looked up and smiled. "I was wondering when you would be up."

"Good morning," he told her before nodding at Benjamin. "Morning."

Based on the cool look Benjamin gave him, the guy still wasn't happy about their conversation last night. They would have to deal with that later. First, there were a few things Colton needed to review with Elise.

"I meant to ask you last night," Colton said as he took a seat. "Did you get up with Tara Campbell's boyfriend?"

Benjamin shifted in his seat. "I did talk to him . . . but he clammed up. I tried some different tactics to get him to talk, but none of them worked. Honestly, he seemed spooked."

Colton rubbed his jaw. "That makes me think he knows something."

"Me too."

Colton would have to think of a different way to

reach the man. "Do you mind if I steal Elise from you for a few minutes? I have a few questions for her."

"Of course." Benjamin stood. "I was just going to take off. I'm going to go work out unless there's something else you need me to do."

"No, feel free. We'll have a meeting at ten."

"I'll be here."

Colton watched him walk out the door. His gaze followed Benjamin through the windows until the man disappeared from sight.

"What's up between you two?" Elise stood, her questioning and perceptive gaze on Colton.

"What do you mean?" He thought he hid his feelings better than he actually did, obviously.

"The tension was so thick you could cut it with a knife."

"Just work stuff."

"You know what Daniel always said. It's best to get things out in the open, to fight it out, and then let things return to normal."

"I always thought that was good advice," Colton said. "But we all work things out in our own ways."

"Yes, we do." Elise ran a finger over the rim of her coffee mug. "You said there was something that you wanted to talk to me about."

"I do. Want to take a walk and talk?"

She nodded. "I'd love that. Let me get my shoes. It's a little too cold to go barefoot."

Five minutes later, they were strolling across the sand as waves crashed beside them. Elise shoved her hands deep into her pockets, looking like she was trying to stay warm. It was cold outside, but not as cold as it had been.

"So what's going on?" she asked.

"I've been attempting to review who could be behind this. Really, our pool of suspects should be very small." He paced beside her, their steps slow and leisurely. "I feel like there's something we're missing here."

"I'll do anything I can to help. Of course. What do you need to know?"

"There aren't that many people who know you discovered this information. I was hoping that you could review with me again what you did after you found that go-bag belonging to Daniel."

"Of course." Elise sucked in a long breath and stared off into the distance for a moment. "I found it and looked at everything. It was probably an hour before I decided I had to tell somebody what I had found. I thought about calling you first, but I didn't know where you were or if you wanted to talk to me."

If you wanted to talk to me? What did that even mean? If this was a different conversation, Colton would've asked. But right now, he needed to stay focused.

"So it only made sense that I would call the command. Brian answered—"

"Who's Brian?"

"He's the commander's assistant," Elise said. "He's worked for him for years. Nice guy."

"Right. Go on."

"Brian answered the phone and patched me through to Commander Larson. I told him that I had found something belonging to Daniel, and I thought he should know about it."

"What did he say?" Colton asked.

"He said I should bring it down to the command, to his office."

"So, at that point, either the commander or Brian Starks may have heard that you found something?"

Elise shrugged. "I don't think Brian would've heard anything, but I suppose it's a possibility. But you also said there was a chance that either my house or my phone had been bugged."

"Yes, that's correct. However, if that's true, then our pool of suspects is much larger than we thought." Colton rubbed his chin, not liking that thought. But it was a possibility. "When did the commander tell you to bring it in?"

"As soon as I could. However, I had a full caseload that day, so we agreed to meet the next morning instead."

"What did you do with the information in the meantime?"

"I took pictures of all of it and I saved it on that SD card. I hid the originals somewhere they wouldn't be found."

"I realize you may not want to tell me, but was the information in your house? Not to sound crass, but did it burn up with the rest of your place?"

"No, I made sure I took it somewhere other than my house."

Colton felt a surge of admiration rush through him. "Smart girl. Okay, keep going."

"As I was driving in to meet him the next morning, he called me and asked me if I would meet him outside. He'd just been called to a meeting, but he wanted to hear what I had to say. When I got to the command and parked, he met me in a limo as I was about to walk into the building."

"A limo?"

"He was meeting with the Secretary of the Navy. It was his limo."

"So you got into the limo with them?"

"That's correct. We only had a couple minutes of general chitchat before I told him what I found."

"Did you pass anybody else in that process?"

"The only other person in that car was the driver, but there was a shield up between the front and the back of the vehicle. I'm assuming he couldn't hear."

"Good job, Elise. That's what I needed to know."

"I didn't tell anybody else about it, but I had a bad feeling. Part of me wasn't even surprised when that man showed up at my house that night before I fled. My gut told me that something was askew. I came here, and now you and your men and Ty know about it. But there's nobody else."

Colton felt his jaw tighten again.

"So, if I'm reading between the lines correctly, you think that the culprit here might be someone associated with either one of your guys, the commander, or the Secretary of the Navy?" Elise asked.

"I don't want to admit that any of that is true, but it is a possibility."

Just then, someone called out and jogged toward them.

Dez.

Colton paused, his gut telling him that something was up.

"You'll never believe this," Dez started, pausing beside them. "I just tried to call my friend Kari."

"The cryptologist?"

"That's right. I wanted to hear if she had any updates on that code."

"And?" Colton asked.

Dez shook his head. "She was in a car accident last night. She's . . . dead."

CHAPTER TWENTY-FOUR

ELISE COULDN'T GET Dez's announcement out of her mind as she washed the dishes from breakfast. She didn't know this Kari woman, but it was no coincidence she was dead. Colton obviously didn't think so either. He'd been on the phone since they got back to the cottage.

Whatever that code said, someone was desperate to keep it hidden.

This kept getting worse and worse, didn't it?

As she dried her last dish, Elise heard the footsteps coming up the steps. She paused and craned her neck to see who was here now. Across the room, she saw Colton tense and start to rise.

It was only Cassidy.

The woman waved a quick hello before wandering over to Elise.

"How are you feeling today?" Cassidy casually crossed her arms and leaned against the kitchen counter.

"I'm doing okay. Why? Is something wrong?"

"I just paid a visit to Henry Adams."

"How is he doing this morning?"

"He left the clinic, refused to stay. Our island doctor thinks Henry needs more help, but he wasn't able to commit him."

"If the man is suicidal, I would definitely agree with that assessment. Can you take him to a bigger hospital with more resources?"

"Apparently, legally, we cannot. But Henry is asking to talk to you."

Elise cut off the water and dried her hands.

"He wants to talk to me?" she repeated, uncertain if she had heard correctly.

Cassidy nodded. "That's correct. He thinks you can help him. You have absolutely no obligation to do this, but—"

"I will." Elise nodded, certainty in her voice.

"Are you sure that's a good idea?" Colton asked, stepping into the conversation.

"He doesn't appear to be a danger to anybody except himself," Elise said. "I don't see where this could hurt anything."

"I feel obligated to remind you that he had a gun yesterday, and he could have cost someone his life when he fell from the pier and had to be rescued," Cassidy said.

"I know. I still would like to talk to him, though." Elise paused. "Was the gun his?"

"Yes, it was registered to him. He doesn't have a criminal record or even a parking ticket, for that matter."

"I don't want you to go by yourself," Colton said. "If you go, I'm going with you. I don't care about patient confidentiality."

Elise pushed a hair behind her ear. "Since he is not officially my patient, that shouldn't be a problem. Besides, I would feel better if you were there with me."

Colton nodded, but his muscles still looked tight. "Do you see any problems with that, Cassidy?"

"I would feel a lot better if you were there also. I've got to go manage some of the protesters again, or I'd go myself."

"Are they at it again today?"

"The surveyor is here. We tried not to let word leak, but somehow it did anyway."

Colton nodded. "Do you want me to send a couple of my guys over to help you?"

"There are only about twenty people out today, so we should be fine. But I'll call if we need you."

"Sounds good."

After rattling off the address, Cassidy grabbed an apple from the counter and went out the door again.

Elise glanced at Colton. "Let me get cleaned up a little, and then we can go."

COLTON KNEW he was probably being overly cautious, but the fewer people Elise came in contact with, the better. Still, he knew that Elise had a heart for helping hurting people. There was no way she wouldn't offer her services to someone in need.

A few minutes later, he pulled up to a small cottage one block from the ocean. The place was nothing fancy, but the outside looked neat and clean. Colton stayed close to Elise as they walked up the set of stairs to the entrance.

Before they could even knock, the door flew open and Henry stood there. He blinked when he saw Colton beside Elise.

"I asked for her, not you." Henry puckered his face as if he'd eaten something sour.

"We are a package deal right now." Colton's voice left no room for argument.

Elise rested a hand on his chest, as if telling him to take a deep breath. Then she glanced back at Henry. "I'm not doing anything without Colton right now. So it's either both of us or neither of us."

Henry stared at them a moment before saying, "Fine. Come in."

They stepped inside the outdated cottage with old brown carpet and dark paneled walls. Colton wasn't one to be a snob when it came to decorating, but there was something about the cave-like atmosphere of this place that felt depressing.

Henry sat in one of the chairs and directed the two of them to sit on the couch across from him. The man seemed to be in better spirits today. Still anxious, but not quite as frantic or melancholy.

Elise leaned toward him, her elbows resting on her knees and her hands laced together in a conversational manner. "How are you doing today, Henry? I know yesterday was a rough day, to say the least."

"I don't know how I'm doing today. I want to believe that everything is going to get better, but I'm just not sure I can."

"Why do you think that nothing will get better?" she asked.

"Because it hasn't yet."

"There's a big difference between not yet and later," Elise said. "Sometimes these things just need some space."

Colton had always been impressed by the wisdom Elise exuded. She seemed capable of calming the most uptight of people. She even had that effect on Colton sometimes.

Her words echoed in his mind. *There's a big different between not yet and later.* Could that be true for him also? Since Daniel's death, he'd felt that his life had been on pause. Like he would never get past that moment.

But what if his future still had a "not yet"?

"What should I do about my wife?" he asked. "I love her more than anything in the whole world."

Elise tilted her head, almost as if she hadn't expected that question. "When was the last time the two of you spoke?"

"It's been a week."

"Where is she now?"

"I don't know."

Elise nodded slowly, thoughtfully. "Tell me about her."

Henry talked about how they'd met. How she was a schoolteacher. Said she was the most loving person he'd ever met.

Elise listened and asked questions to get more of the story from him.

As Colton glanced around, his gaze came to a stop at something protruding from beneath one of the chair cushions.

Was that a gun?

Suddenly, this meeting seemed like a terrible idea.

CHAPTER TWENTY-FIVE

ELISE FELT she was just starting to make progress when Colton nudged her. At first, she wanted to ignore him. Then she realized Colton would only interrupt if he had a good reason. What did he know that she didn't?

She rubbed her hands on her pants and stood. "I'm glad we've been able to talk today, Henry. I'd be happy to talk to you again sometime, but unfortunately right now our time is up. I need to go."

He jumped to his feet. "Time is up? I didn't realize we were working on a time schedule. I'm not ready for you to leave yet. We only just started."

Colton grasped her arm and nudged himself in front of her. "Sorry, but Elise has other things that she needs to attend to."

As they stepped toward the door, Henry stuck his foot in front of it. "No. Don't go."

Colton bristled beside Elise. "I don't think you understand. We're leaving."

The next instant, the man pulled a gun—a second one—from his pocket and swung it out in front of them.

"You don't understand. No one is leaving here. Not until I say they do."

Elise gasped. Was Henry the one who had been behind the threats against her the whole time?

She hadn't seen it coming. If that was true, why would this man have gone to the trouble of pretending to want to kill himself yesterday? It didn't make sense.

All Elise could see right now was the gun that he pointed at them.

"You both need to sit down." His nostrils flared. "Right now."

COLTON SUCKED IN A BREATH. He knew he could take this man. But he wasn't sure he was ready to chance that yet. He couldn't risk Elise somehow getting hurt in the process.

"What do you want from us, Henry?" Colton didn't take his eyes off the man. He'd known Henry was unstable, but he hadn't expected this.

"I'm supposed to kill you." Sweat sprinkled across his upper lip.

Elise gasped beside him. "Kill me? Why would you kill me?"

"If I don't, Alice is going to die."

Colton didn't like the sound of that. "What do you mean?"

"Someone abducted her as she left work. I got a phone call telling me to come here. That I should wait for more instructions. Then this person told me I needed to have a mental health crisis. In public. And ask for help. Going to the pier and pretending like I wanted to take my own life was the only thing I could think of."

Colton's mind raced. Had the caller assumed that if Henry had a mental breakdown then Elise would be called to the scene? It seemed like a pretty big assumption. Then, again, maybe this person knew Elise well enough to know she had a heart for helping people.

That didn't make Colton feel any better.

"What else did this caller say?" The tremble in Elise's voice revealed a touch of fear.

"He told me you were my target. Said you were on the island and you were a psychologist. I needed to stage something where you might come and then I needed to kill you. I could make it look like an accident. Whatever I wanted."

"So you went to the pier yesterday," Colton clarified. He didn't like the sound of any of this. "Elise just happened to come help the police."

"That's right. But I couldn't kill her. I just couldn't. After I fell into the water and was saved, I thought maybe I would have a second chance at all of this. Maybe I could make things right. But then I got another call today."

"What did this person say this time?" Colton asked.

"He said I needed to finish what I was supposed to do yesterday or else. This caller . . . he knew everything about me. He put Alice on the phone. She sounded so scared. I don't know what else to do." His shoulders caved in a silent sob.

"Killing Elise won't fix anything."

Sweat sprinkled across Henry's face. "I don't know what to do. I just want this all to go away."

"You're not a killer, Henry," Elise said. "I think you know that."

"What else am I supposed to do? I can't let Alice die."

"Henry, you need to put the gun down," Colton said. "We can talk about other ways to get Alice back."

"He's right, you know," Elise said. "I know you feel like everything is falling apart right now. But you know this isn't the answer."

"But Alice . . ."

The man stood and waved his gun through the air again. "I just need to end this."

As the man pulled the trigger, Colton threw Elise to the floor, his body covering hers.

Colton glanced back and saw Henry aim the gun at them again. Colton kicked his leg, and the gun flew from Henry's hand.

But Colton knew the man had another weapon.

Jumping to his feet, Colton tackled Henry.

Just as he pinned the man on the floor, the door flew open.

Cassidy rushed inside, gun drawn. "Police!"

It looked like this was over.

But Colton had even more questions than he'd had before.

CHAPTER TWENTY-SIX

AN HOUR LATER, Elise and Colton were in the police station, giving their official statements. Cassidy had stepped out of the room to talk to Henry and left the two of them to take a breather.

Elise was relieved when Cassidy returned to her office and shut the door behind her.

"Any luck figuring out who made these threats?" Colton asked.

"Henry isn't talking. He almost seems comatose, for that matter."

"How did you know to come?" Elise asked. "I thought you were at the protest."

"I was, but I made some phone calls while I was there. In fact, I started looking into Henry's background. I decided to call the school and talk to Henry's wife. The principal said she hadn't been in for four days and that was unlike her. I talked to one of her coworkers who said the same thing. I figured there was more to the story. Just as I pulled up to the house, I heard the gunfire."

"Smart thinking," Colton said.

"You too." Cassidy nodded. "Now, tell me again what he told you."

They ran through what had happened.

Cassidy's frown grew deeper and deeper with every new detail. "Someone wanted to use Henry to kill you. No longer do they want you to hand over the information. I don't want to mince words here, not given how serious this situation is. It sounds like they want to eliminate you now."

Colton tensed beside Elise. He knew just as well as Elise did that Cassidy's words were true. The stakes had just risen—in the worst way possible.

"The person behind this is getting other people to do his dirty work, probably so he won't be discovered himself," Cassidy continued. "So let's just assume that the same person who threatened him is the person threatening you. How did this person connect that you were here?"

"That's a great question." Elise pushed a hair from her eyes and frowned. "I have no idea. I have never seen Henry before. I guess he was supposed to ask for me at the pier, but I showed up before he could. It was supposed to look like an accident."

"That explains why he brought the gun when he was going to jump from the pier," Colton said.

"Yes, that didn't quite make sense, did it? It's safe to say that whoever's behind this has some pretty deep connections." Cassidy frowned and bounced her pen against her desk as she thought. "I believe it. Someone would have to be very connected in order to make all of this happen. They would have to be here looking for a scapegoat, looking for someone they could get to do their bidding. I don't like the sound of this."

"Neither do I," Elise said.

"I want to assure you that we are going to check this guy's phone records, talk to the neighbors, to his colleagues," Cassidy said. "We will do everything we can to get to the bottom of this."

"I appreciate that," Elise said. "Just when I think it can't get worse it does."

Cassidy frowned. "I know what that's like. But you guys are free to go for now. I will be in touch if I need anything."

But before they could even stand to leave, someone knocked at the door. Ty stuck his head inside, and his gaze went to Elise. "There's something you need to see."

COLTON BRACED himself for whatever Ty had to say. Based on the look on his face, it wasn't good.

Colton was worried about Elise. How much could a person take before life beat them down and stole the little bit of hope that was left?

He knew Elise better than that, though. She was a fighter. Still, he couldn't help but feel for her.

"What is it?" Elise's voice wavered as she waited for Ty's response.

He held up his phone. "I've been keeping an eye on all the news articles from up in Virginia Beach. Especially after you told me about the house fire. This article came out today, and it's about you."

Elise took his outstretched phone, but her hands trembled so badly that the screen was impossible to read. Colton took the device from her and held it out in front of them both.

He scanned the words there, and his muscles tightened with every new sentence.

It was an article about Elise. Her picture was on the front page. There were smaller pictures of her house fire and also one of a man Colton didn't recognize.

Elise let out a soft cry beside him. He wasn't sure exactly what was going through her head, but Colton put an arm around her shoulders and pulled her closer.

She buried her head in his chest. "Bernie is dead."

"Who is Bernie?" Colton asked.

"He was my neighbor. They found his body in my house. He was the nicest man. He didn't deserve this."

"When was the last time you saw him?"

"Probably the day before I left. He was always trying to be helpful. Bringing me my newspaper or vegetables from the farmer's market. I bet he heard me scream that night I was attacked. While I was running, he probably came over to check on me and got caught in this whole mess." A muted sob escaped.

"It's not your fault, Elise." Colton held her closer.

Cassidy frowned at Elise, her eyes softening, before turning back to Colton and Ty. "What else does the article say?"

The two men exchanged a look before Colton finally nodded and spoke. "It says that Elise is facing accusations about her psychology practice as well. It spells out some of those allegations, and they match those that were sent in that text to her. It also says that she is believed to be on the run right now and possibly armed and dangerous. Anyone with information on her whereabouts is supposed to call the police with information."

Colton's back muscles threaded with tension. People here on this island had seen Elise. Would one of them report her?

"That doesn't sound good." Cassidy's brow furrowed.

Elise lifted her head, her haggard gaze on Cassidy. "Are you obligated to report me?"

Cassidy frowned, her face still tight. "I should. But I also know you're not guilty and that whoever is behind this has some connections."

They all waited, anxious to hear what Cassidy would decide.

Finally, she released her breath and turned toward them, a firm, decisive look in her gaze. "I'm going to give this a day. Let's see if we can figure out some answers. I don't believe that turning you in is going to solve anything. I can't pretend that I didn't see this article, but I am going to choose not to act on it right now."

"Thank you." Elise's voice came out just above a whisper.

Cassidy's gaze met Elise's, and she softened her voice. "I know what it's like to need people to be in your corner. I'll do everything within my power to help you out."

Colton rubbed Elise's arm. She was right. This was just getting worse by the minute.

CHAPTER TWENTY-SEVEN

ELISE WAS STILL DAZED as she and Colton headed from the police station. Whoever was behind this had carried through with his threat. He'd made it seem like Elise was guilty of having an inappropriate relationship with one of her patients. He'd also made it look like she'd had some type of mental break, shot her neighbor, and then burned her house down to cover up the crime.

It wasn't that different from what they had done to Henry. They had threatened him, and Elise had almost lost her life as a result.

The person behind this was soulless. No other explanation made sense. The question that remained in Elise's mind was just what was he trying to hide? Why was this information that Daniel had found so important?

Colton remained quiet beside her, but she knew the thoughts turning over in his mind reflected hers. He didn't like this any more than she did.

As she reached the front door and Colton pulled it open, a wintry wind swept over her. She pulled her coat closer and reminded herself that she'd need to get some new clothes soon, especially since she didn't know how long she would be staying.

As she stepped forward, Elise collided with somebody heading into the police station. She muttered, "So sorry."

Colton froze beside her.

Elise looked up in time to see him scrutinizing the man whose shoulder had bumped hers. Her gaze swerved back toward the stranger. She didn't remember seeing him before, but Colton obviously recognized the man.

"You . . ." the man muttered. "I told you I wasn't going to let you get away with this."

"Get away with what?" Colton asked. "I was hired to do a job, and I did it."

"You're not one of us here."

"You're right." Colton straightened. "I'm not. But that doesn't mean I can't live here on Lantern Beach."

The man poked a finger into Colton's chest.

Elise froze, waiting for Colton's reaction. That was a bad move.

"You don't want to touch me," Colton seethed, his voice and gaze hardening.

The man stared at him a moment as if reconsidering. Finally, he lowered his arm. "I'm working hard to ensure that you and your men will not have a headquarters here anymore."

The breath left Elise's lungs. "What? Why would you do that?"

There was obviously more to the story than she knew.

"Having an organization like Blackout here is risky," the man said. "Too risky. It's bringing trouble to this island, and trouble isn't what we need."

"How are we bringing trouble to the island?" Colton's jaw visibly tightened.

"For starters, there was that speeding ticket one of your guys got."

"He admitted that he was going too fast and paid his fine," Colton said. "It's not the first time someone has been caught speeding on this island. I can assure you of that."

"When you guys helped to take down that cult that was here, it brought too much attention to the island. There were too many articles. And now thrill-seekers are trying to come here, as well as hotel developers. I don't like it."

Colton stepped forward. "Look, I don't know what

your beef is with me, but I'm not the guy you need to come after."

"We'll see about that." The man raised his chin and stepped into the police station.

When he was out of earshot, Elise turn to Colton. "What was that about?"

Colton rubbed his jaw again. "That man—his name is Ron Davis—is one of the biggest employers on Lantern Beach. He runs a management service for the rentals on the island. The hotel that they're talking about putting in is threatening his bottom line. He's afraid it will take away from his own business, so he's fighting with everything in him to make it stop."

"So why is he taking it out on you?"

"I happened to be in front of him when he was at the protest the other day. I wouldn't let him pass, and he didn't seem to appreciate that. From what I understand, he's a local and he has a lot of clout around here."

"You think he will really carry through with his threat?"

"I don't see where Blackout has done anything wrong that would give the town any grounds to get rid of us."

A bad feeling remained in Elise's stomach. The look in that man's eyes had been one of determination. He wanted someone to pay for the potential upheaval in his life.

"It's been quite the day, huh?" Colton said. "Let's get you back home."

But as Colton said the words, his gaze caught someone across the street. "Elise, go inside and stay with Cassidy and Ty. There's someone I need to talk to."

COLTON RAN across the street to the gas station. A familiar figure pumped gas—the man he'd seen with Jason at the pier. The one who'd acted suspicious and had hair like a shark fin.

The man's presence on the island might be a coincidence. But Colton wanted to find out for sure.

"Excuse me!" Colton jogged over to him.

The man's eyes widened when he saw Colton approaching. "Can I help you?"

"I noticed that you weren't from around here." Colton stopped near him but remained a comfortable distance away, as to not spook the man.

"That's right. Is that a problem?" The man's words were short and clipped, as if he didn't appreciate the interruption.

"A problem? No, of course not. But I saw you talking to my friend Jason on the pier yesterday, and that got me curious."

The man glanced at the numbers on the gas pump,

as if checking to see how much longer he had until his tank was full. "It's not a crime to talk to strangers."

"No, but you seem out of place around here. You seemed out of place on the pier, and you seem out of place talking to someone who's homeless. Are those snap judgments? Yes, they are. But when you put it all together, you've got me curious."

"It's none of your business." The man's eyes narrowed.

"Someone I know almost got shot today, so I'm making things my business."

"I'm sorry to hear about your friend." The man put the gas nozzle back into the pump and turned the cap on his gas tank. He moved so quickly that it took three tries to get the cap on straight. "But I really have no idea what you think this has to do with me."

"Because every stranger here on the island is now suspect in my mind."

He snorted. "If you think I'm trying to hurt someone, then you're dead wrong."

"If you're so innocent, why are you acting so shady right now?"

The man let out a sigh and crossed his arms. "Look, if you must know, I'm a developer. Sean Burns is the name."

"You're not the guy who's trying to buy the old campground where Gilead's Cove was." Colton had seen that man, and they were clearly not the same person.

"No, I'm not that guy. But I am interested in buying the land. I'm giving that jerk Damien Marks some competition."

"Wait, so you're with a different hotel?" Colton shifted.

"That's correct. My company has done our market research, and we think that Lantern Beach would be a great place to expand. Everyone's talking about this area."

"And why is that?"

"After all the drama that happened last year with that cult, it's put this place on the map. You know most of the houses here are already booked for the summer and even into the fall. You're running out of places for people to stay here. A hotel would be the answer everyone's looking for."

"You have to understand that the infrastructure isn't set up here yet to accommodate that many people. We would need new roads, more ditches, more water."

"And we can provide all of that." The man straightened. "Look, I don't want to argue with you. I just want to let you know that I'm not the guy that you were looking for."

"Just one more question then," Colton said. "If you came here trying to build a hotel, why were you talking to the homeless man yesterday? How does that tie in?"

Sean looked into the distance and let out a long breath before turning back to Colton. "Because I want him to be the poster boy for affordable housing. People who make less than $50,000 a year can't find a decent place to live around here. They are trying to live at campgrounds instead."

"How would a hotel help?"

"We'd offer weekly rates that would be cheaper than most of the mortgages people can get on this island—even cheaper in the off season. Our prices would make it possible for them to have a room, even year-round if that's what they want."

"Sounds more like an apartment complex."

"But it's not. There's no contract. Year-round residents and guests alike can use it."

His explanation sounded reasonable, but Colton still remained on guard. "I see. How long are you going to be in town?"

"I'm planning on leaving in the morning. Now, if you don't mind." Sean pointed to his driver's side seat.

Colton nodded and started back toward the police station. He had more answers now. But he still didn't have enough answers.

CHAPTER TWENTY-EIGHT

"IF YOU DON'T MIND me asking, what was that about?" Elise asked as she and Colton headed back toward Ty and Cassidy's cottage.

"I saw someone that I spotted on the pier yesterday. He seemed out of place in this area, so I wondered..."

"If he had something to do with the threats against me," Elise finished.

"Exactly."

"And did he?" She held her breath as she waited to hear what Colton had found out.

"He's interested in possibly building a hotel here and giving Damien Marks some competition. He's a shrewd businessman, but he appears to have nothing to do with what's going on with you."

"At least you know now."

"That's right. At least I know."

They pulled up to the cottage, parked, and started up the steps at a slow, unhurried pace. As they did, Elise's thoughts wandered to the future. Was this where Colton planned on staying and putting down roots? Did he see Blackout as a permanent part of his future?

"How long are you guys going to use Ty's place?" she finally asked.

"We don't have the funding yet to get a place of our own, but I know we are going to outgrow this quickly. As nice as it is that Ty and Cassidy are letting us use their home, I know they are going to want their privacy soon. Especially if they have kids one day. No one wants a bunch of former Navy SEALs hanging out in their house and plotting missions with toddlers running around."

"Well, I hope that you are able to find something. Do you want to stay here in Lantern Beach?"

"That's the plan. I like it here. I like that we can come back here to regroup and take a load off after adrenaline-pumping missions. There's something really peaceful about being here. I mean, when there aren't murders, cults, or protests."

Elise flashed a smile. "Well said."

He glanced at his watch as they reached the screened-in porch. "My guys are supposed to be here any minute. We need to regroup. Would you like to join us?"

"I would love to. I want to figure this out more than anyone."

A few minutes later they were all seated in the living room. They relayed everything they had just learned and experienced to the rest of the group.

"What we really need here right now are some suspects," Colton said.

For the next two hours, they talked about suspects.

Leonardo—suspicious timing.

Jason—also suspicious timing.

Henry—could be more to his story.

Brian Starks—he had access to the command.

After they'd discussed things ad nauseam, Colton could tell everyone was tired.

Maybe the best thing they could do right now was to take a little breather.

He stood. "Let's take fifteen minutes to stretch our legs or get something to drink. And then I want to meet back here again so we can finish talking about all these clues. Got it?"

A round of nods and affirmations went around the circle. As Colton glanced at Elise again, his heart sank. He wished he could do something to relieve some of the burden she'd been carrying.

Instead, he held out his hand toward her. "Would you like to step outside a minute for some fresh air?"

"I'd love some."

They didn't have time to go far. Instead, they

stepped onto the screened-in porch and stood beside each other near the cedar-shingled wall. Darkness had fallen around them, concealing the beautiful ocean scenery. But the change in environment was nice.

He had to admit that the break was nice for him also—especially if he could spend it with Elise.

But that thought was just as dangerous as the mission in front of him.

ELISE DREW IN A DEEP BREATH. That meeting had been a lot to take in. There was so much information yet so few leads, it seemed.

Either way, she was grateful to be out here now.

"I was always a little jealous of Daniel, you know," Colton said.

Elise turned toward him, her heart thrumming in her ears. "Why's that?"

"Because I thought he'd found the perfect girl."

She let out a little laugh. "You thought I was the perfect girl?"

He shrugged quickly before staring off in the distance. "Yeah, I did. You fiercely defended him. You stuck with him when the going got tough, you put him in his place when he needed it, and you had his back at other times."

It was her turn to shrug now. "I did my best. I was far from perfect, though."

She could feel Colton's eyes on her.

"What are you thinking?" he asked.

"I guess, ever since I found that hidden box, I wonder about how life might have been different if Daniel hadn't died in that training exercise. If the two of us had gotten away and started a new life together somewhere else. Somewhere we'd be able to spend time together."

Colton's hand covered her shoulder. "I don't know the answer to that question. Is that what you wish had happened? That you and Daniel were off somewhere together right now?"

"That wouldn't have erased our problems." She licked her lips. "Besides, there's no need to dwell on the what ifs. That's what I always tell my patients."

"But sometimes it's human nature to do so."

She turned to him, feeling her breath catch. "You're right. It is human nature. We all try to deal with tragedy in our own ways."

"Yes, we do."

Their gazes caught.

Elise licked her lips. Before she could talk herself out of it, she said, "You know, I always thought Daniel was pretty lucky to have you as a best friend."

Colton raised an eyebrow. "I thought I was a bad influence."

"You were the best kind of bad influence. You helped pull him from his intensity. Helped him see other viewpoints. He knew he could always count on you."

Something flooded his gaze. A new emotion. Was that guilt?

"Daniel's death wasn't your fault, you know," she said quietly.

"It feels like it was my fault."

"We always want things to make sense. Did you know that's why we so often see pictures in clouds or make up stories out of constellations? It's our basic human nature to want answers and reasons. But sometimes there just isn't any reason to be found. We have to be able to accept that."

Colton pushed a hair away from her face, his gaze nearly mesmerizing her. "You're a pretty smart lady, Elise."

"You're a pretty brave man, Colton."

Before either of them could say anything else, an unseen force seemed to draw them closer. Closer. Closer.

Finally, their lips met. Electricity exploded between them, and fire seemed to burn across her skin as Colton's hand went to her waist.

Just as quickly as the kiss had begun, they both stepped back and stared at each other.

"What do you think Daniel would think about

that?" Colton's voice sounded gravelly with emotion as he stared at her, their faces only inches apart.

"I think he'd want us both to be happy." Elise wanted to believe that. Deep inside, she did. Then why did she feel guilty?

"I want to tell you that I won't even entertain the thought of doing that again if you say the word," Colton said. "But I'm not sure I'd be telling the truth."

Something about the sly smile on his face, about the sparkle in his eyes, got Elise's blood pumping in a way she hadn't felt in years. "I would never ask you to do that."

He tugged her closer again until their bodies were next to each other.

Elise almost didn't want to believe it, didn't want to risk it, but . . . was it possible that she might have a second chance at love?

CHAPTER TWENTY-NINE

ELISE FELT FLUSHED. Had she really just kissed Colton? And had it really felt that good?

She knew the answer. No doubt, it was a yes.

But every time she remembered how much she enjoyed it, an equal amount of guilt trickled into her mind. Why did she feel like she was betraying Daniel? He wasn't here anymore. Still, the guilt was surprisingly strong.

Colton rubbed the sides of her arms. "Maybe we should get back inside. I think my sanctioned break time is over. Obviously, I should've made it longer."

Elise smiled, reluctant to leave the moment, yet desperate to get away. The two emotions collided with each other inside her.

"Next time, take a longer break."

A soft smile played on his lips. He opened his

mouth, looking as if he wanted to say more. Before he could, someone tapped on the window.

Dez. Good old Dez.

Colton dropped his hand from her arm, though the motion almost seemed reluctant. "We can talk more later."

Elise smiled. Talking wasn't exactly what she was thinking about. But talking was a good thing, especially considering the scope of what had just happened. They would need to figure out which direction they should go after this.

She wiped her lips, hoping to remove any evidence of the kiss. She wasn't ready for everyone to know their business. Instead, Elise tried to compose herself as Colton ushered her back inside.

She took a seat and leaned back, trying to focus on the talk at hand. Yet all her thoughts wanted to do was go back to that kiss.

It had been so long since she felt the giddiness she did now. She and Daniel had had that once, but they had drifted apart over the years and sometimes the divide between them had felt insurmountable. Elise had hoped for reconciliation and for happier days. But they never got a chance to work out their issues.

And now Colton was here . . .

"Did anyone have any other thoughts while we were on our break?" Colton asked.

No one said anything for a moment. Finally,

Benjamin shifted. He glanced at Colton and then at Elise.

"I think we should tell her what really happened," he announced.

As soon as the sentence left his lips, tension thick enough to crackle filled the room.

What in the world was Benjamin talking about?

She swung her head toward Colton. "What does that mean?"

Colton narrowed his gaze at Benjamin, who shrugged.

"I think she deserves to know," Benjamin repeated. "I don't care if it's supposed to be classified. I'm not a SEAL anymore, and I'm tired of covering things up."

"Colton," Elise said. "Tell me what's going on."

Colton ran a hand over his face and his shoulders seemed to droop. When his gaze met hers, the emotions in his eyes were tumultuous at best. Guilty at worst.

"I'm so sorry, Elise." His voice cracked. "I've wanted to tell you for the past year. But Daniel didn't die during a training exercise. He died during a black ops mission."

"What?"

He nodded. "And it was all my fault."

ELISE FELT the air leave her lungs. "What? What are you talking about?"

All of the guys exchanged glances. There was obviously a lot more going on here than she knew. Though she'd always suspected that there was more to the story of Daniel's death, she had no idea he was involved in black ops missions.

"We were sent to ambush Manuel Tersoo," Colton started. "We had good intel that he was on a fishing boat. He was using it to cover his whereabouts as he headed to France. We believe he was going there to meet with an investor and to sell the tantalum his men had been stealing."

"Okay . . ." Elise waited for the story to continue.

"But someone knew we were coming," Colton said. "We'd been double-crossed. As soon as we showed up on that boat, they were waiting. We were all supposed to die that night."

"That's terrible."

"All of it was off-books. No one was supposed to know. In fact, there was a whole cover story about how an opposing terrorist group would be blamed. If we were caught, the government wasn't sending anyone for us."

"What happened?" The words burned as they left her throat.

"We had to abort the mission. It was Daniel's call.

He knew all of our lives were on the line. As he was trying to get us off the boat, he was shot."

Elise's hand covered her mouth, and she muffled a cry. She tried not to picture everything happening, but how could she not?

"I was supposed to have his back." Colton's voice cracked again. "I should have seen that shooter before the bullet ever reached Daniel."

"We all should have," Dez's face looked just as grim as the rest of the group.

"What happened to him?" Elise's gaze scanned each person in the group. "Why didn't you bring his body back?"

"We couldn't find it," Griff said. "We searched for days and days. We even went back on our own, without the military knowing. We couldn't find it anywhere."

"Do you think the Savages found it?"

"If they did, they haven't owned up to it," Benjamin said. "Usually a group like that will want to brag. They never did. Most likely, the ocean claimed it."

Elise stood, not wanting anyone to see her tears as betrayal flooded her chest cavity. "I'm going to need a moment."

Colton stood and reached for her, but she stepped away before he could touch her. "Elise..."

"I just need . . . I just need time. I knew when Daniel became a SEAL that there would be missions I could never know the details on. But this . . . it's turned everything I thought about his death upside down. I'm going to need time to process this."

Before anyone could say anything else, she escaped to her room.

So many people thought her husband had died a traitor. In truth, he was a hero.

How could Elise even try to feel happy while knowing her husband had been denied justice? It seemed... like a disgrace.

CHAPTER THIRTY

COLTON FELT anger bristling his muscles as his gaze fell on Benjamin. "Why in the world did you think it was a good idea to pull that stunt?"

Benjamin rose to his full height, defiance in his gaze. "Because Elise deserved to know the truth."

"That wasn't your decision," Colton seethed.

"You certainly weren't going to make the choice."

"And I had my reasons, starting with the fact that the details are supposed to be classified." Anger simmered in Colton's voice as he fisted his hands at his side.

"He's right," Dez said, his voice low and serious. "You shouldn't have made that call, Benjamin."

Benjamin raised his hands in the air as tension crackled between them. "There's nothing that I can do that will make you guys trust me, is there?"

"There are boundaries in place," Griff said. "You just crossed them. Big time."

"Hiding the truth about what happened that night hasn't done us any favors," Benjamin said. "We've all been empty shells since then. What can we say? We were the only Navy SEAL team to ever leave one of our guys behind."

"We tried to find him." Colton's voice rose with emotion. "We did everything in our power to locate Daniel. We even went back to that site three times trying to find him. Finally, the command said we were done. What else were we supposed to do?"

"I'm just saying, don't make me out to be the bad guy here. We all had a hand in what happened there, and, in our own ways, we blame each other for the loss of Daniel, don't we?"

Colton clenched his fists tighter, trying to keep himself in control. "What happened that night was a tragedy. I know we're all dealing with it in our own ways, but you need to take a step back, Benjamin."

"Isn't that what I always do? Take a step back. I've always felt like an outsider. This just proves that I am." His jaw flexed as he shook his head.

"No one said that you were an outsider," Dez said, his voice still calm. "But Elise didn't deserve to find out that way."

"If I didn't say something, no one else would. If it was my spouse who died, I'd want to know the truth."

"I can't talk to you right now," Colton muttered. "There's a part of you that wants to see this team fail, isn't there?"

Benjamin blanched. "Why in the world would I want to see us fail?"

"After Daniel died . . . you were the only one who didn't want to go back and look for his body." Colton grit his teeth at the thought.

The words seemed to wash over Benjamin before he grimaced. "It was one of my first missions. I was shaken up. What can I say?"

"You know we never leave a guy behind." Dez shook his head, not looking entirely happy himself.

Benjamin took a step back. "I know what all of you guys think. You think that I only got this position because my uncle is the Secretary of the Navy."

No one said anything. That thought had crossed Colton's mind. He'd be lying if he said it hadn't.

Still bristling, Benjamin lowered his hands, and his gaze swept around the room, almost as if he waited for someone to defend him. Finally, with one last glance back at them, he stepped out the door and slammed it behind him.

When he was gone, the rest of the team looked at each other.

"It wasn't supposed to go that way." Dez ran a hand over his face.

"No, it wasn't." Colton placed his hands on his hips, anger still simmering in him.

"Do you think Elise is going to be okay?" Griff glanced up from his spot on the couch.

"The news shook her up," Colton said. "I can only imagine what's going through her mind right now."

Colton couldn't help but wonder how this might change their relationship. He knew there were bigger stakes at hand, bigger issues. But part of his heart felt shattered. To finally take that step forward with Elise, only to have everything come crashing down around him...

Colton needed to figure out a way to fix this.

But first he had to figure out who was behind these threats...

ELISE HUGGED the pillow to her chest as the conversation played out in her mind again and again. Tears ran down her cheeks with every new image that entered her mind.

Daniel had died at the hands of a terrorist. His death had been violent. Not an accident.

And she'd been totally in the dark.

She'd been in the dark about so many things.

She'd believed a lie about his death for the past

year. She didn't want to be bothered by the fact. But she was.

A light tap sounded at her door. She wanted to tell whoever was there to go away, but something inside her stopped her. Instead, she called, "Come in."

Colton stuck his head in the room. "Can we talk?"

"Not really feeling much like talking right now." She pulled the pillow closer, feelings clashing inside her. On one hand, Colton had come to mean so much to her. On the other hand, her husband deserved so much more than her running off with his best friend . . . even if Daniel was no longer here.

Colton stepped inside and closed the door. His gaze looked downright tortured. "I know you're not. I just want to say . . . I'm sorry."

She wiped beneath her eyes, trying to hide any evidence of her tears. "So am I."

Colton shoved his hands into his pockets, his shoulders slumped with invisible burdens. "I wanted to tell you, you know."

"I'm sure you did." Elise's voice sounded hollow, almost like she didn't believe the words herself. Maybe she didn't. She wasn't sure yet.

"Is there anything I can do right now?" His eyes implored hers.

"Right now, I just want to be alone. I don't know what any of this means . . . for my future. For us. I need to sort through things. I wish . . . I wish I hadn't found out like that."

"It wasn't supposed to be that way."

"No, if it was up to you, I would've never known, would I?"

She saw Colton flinch and knew her words had hurt. Maybe that was what Elise had intended. She wanted Colton to know how she felt after someone she cared about had betrayed her. Yet another part of her knew that wasn't fair.

She couldn't get her thoughts together.

"I don't know what to say." Colton's voice cracked.

"Then don't say anything. Not now, at least. Now, if you don't mind, I need to be by myself."

Colton nodded and stepped back toward the door. His hand gripped the knob, but his eyes remained on her. "I'm sorry, Elise."

She nodded. But she knew there was a good chance things would never be the same. Ever.

She might be able to forgive Colton. But would she ever be able to forget?

CHAPTER THIRTY-ONE

COLTON DECIDED to sleep in one of the spare bedrooms in the cottage that evening. The evidence Elise had brought with her was now locked in the secure office Ty kept in his home. Colton wanted to spend the evening reviewing each photo again—and he also wanted to be close to Elise, just in case.

Danger felt close—too close—and he didn't want to take any chances.

Anger—and sorrow—still burned through him when he thought about the way things had played out.

Things weren't supposed to happen this way. But the best thing he could do right now was to give Elise some space. He hoped in the morning they could talk.

Sitting at the desk, Colton rubbed his eyes. He had to figure out who was behind this. Failure wasn't an option.

What was he missing?

The burner phone Daniel had left seemed to be a non-lead. The numbers were untraceable.

It was the code and the photos that were their best bet for finding answers.

He began poring over the photos that Daniel had taken. What event was this? Everyone was dressed to the nines.

As he stared at the rooms and décor, he realized the place seemed vaguely familiar. But he couldn't identify why.

What kind of events would draw these crowds of people? The commander? The Secretary of the Navy? Tara Campbell?

Colton got on the computer and began clicking on things. A few minutes later, he had his answer.

These were taken at an art gallery in Norfolk.

An art gallery? Colton wasn't sure that offered him any more answers than he'd had before.

Something about these photos and the people in them were important enough that Daniel had hidden them. It shouldn't be this hard to figure out what.

Colton let out a sigh and leaned back. He ran a hand over his face, fighting frustration over it all.

Maybe he just needed some sleep.

Maybe things would look brighter in the morning.

ELISE FELT like she had just fallen asleep when she heard a buzzing beside her.

She sat up in bed, unaware she'd been sleeping so deeply. She'd been pulled into a dreamlike vortex where she was being chased by a masked man. Now sweat covered her brow, and her sheets felt wet with perspiration.

The buzzing started again.

Her gaze went to her nightstand, and she saw that it was her phone.

A sick feeling formed in her gut. The only person who used this number was the person threatening her. Was that person calling her now?

She glanced at her watch. Two AM.

Elise prayed this was just a wrong number and not another threat.

But she knew better.

With trembling hands, she picked up the phone and put it to her ear. Her throat was dry and scratchy as she answered.

"Leave the house," a deep voice ordered. "Right now."

"Why would I want to do that?" Her voice quivered at the foreshadowing of what was to come.

"I planted tripwire bombs at each of the cabanas and the cottage where you're staying. If you refuse to cooperate, I will be forced to detonate my little toys—I set up a remote option as well. Your friends will be no more."

Elise gasped, instant—and horrifying—pictures filling her mind. Pictures she couldn't bear to visualize.

"What do you want me to do?" she whispered.

"Tell no one where you're going. If I suspect you of slipping up, I'll be forced to take action. I'll test out this remote option on one of the cabanas, just for fun."

She pressed her eyes shut.

"You're going to step out the front door," he continued. "Walk over the sand dune. I'll give you further instructions once you do that. You have five minutes. Not a moment more."

"Won't the bomb go off?"

"I have all that figured out. You just come out."

Sweat scattered across her brow. "I don't have the evidence with me, if that's what you want."

"I want you, Elise. Five minutes."

A chill swept over her, a chill so frigid Elise felt as if she might pass out. Before she could argue or say anything else, the line went dead.

Elise had to make a choice. But she already knew what it was. There was no way she could let her friends get hurt because of her. But that didn't stop the nauseous feeling from rolling around in her stomach.

This was it. When she left this house, Elise would most likely never see these people again.

Even after everything that happened yesterday, the

gang here still felt like family. These people had been there for her.

She glanced at her watch again. It was 2:03 now. She didn't have much time to get outside or the man would take drastic measures.

Elise threw the covers off and pulled her shoes on, along with a coat. She started toward the door but paused. Quickly, she ran back to her dresser, found a pen and paper, and scribbled a quick note. Maybe someone would see this in time.

With one last glance at her room, Elise tiptoed down the hallway. This was it. The moment she should've known was coming.

The moment when the bad guy would win.

Elise only wished she had a little more time to make things right.

Instead, she left the note by the front door and prayed everyone saw it in time.

CHAPTER THIRTY-TWO

ELISE FELT the trembles claim her as she stepped outside. *Please, Lord, help me now.*

She didn't know if she was doing the right thing or not. She only knew that she had to do it. She had no other choice.

A frigid wind swept around her as soon as she paused on the screened porch. It seemed to warn her to run now while she could. Instead, she quietly closed the door behind her, so as to not wake anybody else up.

IEDs . . . that was all she could think about. They had been planted around here somewhere and could detonate at any moment.

She craned her neck and saw the box attached to the door. The blood left her face.

A wire came from the box, over the windows.

The man hadn't been bluffing.

There was a bomb on this house.

She had no assurance that the man wouldn't blow up the house anyway, despite her keeping the promise. But what other choice did she have?

For that matter, how did she know that her next step would be safe? That an explosive hadn't been planted in her path, as well as around the buildings?

That was the thing. She didn't know that. She *couldn't* know.

She hurried down the steps and into the darkness below. Without any streetlights or outdoor lamps, the darkness felt deeper here than in her suburban neighborhood. The blackness unnerved her, took her breath away.

Despite her fear, she climbed the sand dune. Crossed to the beach on the other side. It seemed even darker here, more ominous.

What was next? The man had said he'd give her more directions. But Elise didn't see anyone out here.

Her gaze went to the cabanas in the back of the property. Was Colton sleeping in his bed now, oblivious to all this?

Elise's heart rate sped as she thought about him. Though he'd kept the truth about Daniel's death from her, Elise knew deep down inside that she cared about him. She just needed time to work through her emotions. Would she ever have that chance?

A muted cry lodged in her throat at the thought. If only she could talk to him now. Explain things.

But that wasn't an option.

Elise glanced at her phone. Still nothing.

It's not too late. You can still run back inside and tell somebody.

But Elise knew that she wouldn't do that. Whoever had made these threats against her knew the same thing.

As she began pacing again, she sensed someone behind her.

The next thing she knew, a black bag came down over her head. Before she could scream, a hand covered her mouth. An arm clamped down across her and lifted her from her feet.

"I knew you'd come. Say goodbye to your friends—because this is the end of the road."

CASSIDY AWOKE TO A STRANGE SOUND. What was that?

She nudged Ty beside her. "Wake up. Did you hear that?"

He pushed himself up in bed, his eyes still hazy from sleep. "What?"

"I heard something."

They both paused and listened. Nothing. Silence.

Then . . . she heard it again. "There it is."

"That's just Kujo." Ty ran a hand over his face. "I thought I saw Griff sneaking him some food earlier today. Maybe his stomach is upset."

Cassidy wasn't convinced. "Something is wrong."

"What do you mean?"

"I don't know. I can't put my finger on it. Kujo doesn't usually wake us up. I'm not sure he was the one who woke me. I think it was something else."

"He's scratching at our door right now. He must need to go outside. I'll take care of him." Ty climbed out of bed and threw on some jeans and a T-shirt.

Cassidy knew she wasn't going to be able to stay in bed while Ty checked things out. All of her senses were on alert for some reason. Most likely it was everything that had happened here lately. It put her on edge. But she needed to be certain.

She pulled on a sweatshirt and grabbed the gun from the safe beside her bed.

Ty walked ahead of her in the hallway, speaking in low tones to Kujo. Cassidy glanced up and down the dark corridor but saw nothing out of place. Elise's door was closed. Hopefully, they wouldn't wake her.

Cassidy wandered into the kitchen just as Ty paused by the front door. He leaned down and picked up something on the floor.

"What is it?" Cassidy asked.

Ty's worried gaze met hers. "It's a note. From Elise. We can't open this door. Not if we want to live."

CHAPTER THIRTY-THREE

COLTON HELD the paper in his hands. "You found this note by the door?"

Ty had woken him up with the update about Elise. It still felt surreal.

Cassidy nodded, her face withdrawn and pinched with concern. "Kujo was acting weird, and we knew something was up. By the time we got here, Elise was gone."

They met at the kitchen table. They spoke to Dez and Griff on the phone, and Benjamin . . . he was gone.

"You really think the place is rigged?" Colton asked, trying to think the situation through and keep a cool head.

Ty nodded. "I checked. I can see some kind of box near the handle, and there's a trip wire of some sort over the windows. Based on the amount of C-4 I can see, this whole place could go up in flames."

"And we can't get out the windows either?" Colton asked.

Ty shook his head. "No, we can't. Too bad Benjamin isn't here. He was a bomb tech before he was a SEAL, right?"

Colton nodded. "That's right. That would also make him the perfect person to do this."

Cassidy blinked with obvious surprise. "You think Benjamin could be responsible?"

"He has the means and the opportunity. I just don't want to believe that he has the motivation also."

Cassidy glanced at Ty then Colton. "Then what do we do now? You're talking about things that are a little bit out of my league right now."

"Do you have any bomb-sniffing dogs here on the island?" Colton asked.

"Dane has a dog who's been trained. But he's not here right now. He went over to Hatteras to hang out with a friend last night."

"How long will it take him to get here?"

"The first ferry doesn't leave until seven AM."

"We won't have that kind of time. Can you call him and see if he can get here ASAP? We need to find Elise. Every second she's gone, the less likely it is that we're going to find her."

Alive.

Colton didn't say the last word. But it lingered in his mind.

The less likely it is that we are going to find her alive.

His stomach clenched at the thought.

He couldn't lose someone else on his watch. Not again.

WHOEVER THE MAN was who'd grabbed Elise, he was strong.

He half-carried her, half-shoved her forward. Where was he taking her?

She stumbled over the sand, wanting to struggle. To fight. But it was no use.

This man could clearly overpower her. And, if Elise fought too much, he could set off those bombs.

Finally, they stopped. Something opened, and, the next moment, he shoved Elise into a dark space.

A car trunk. It was the only thing that made sense.

He jerked her hands behind her, and she heard a low-pitched screech.

Duct tape.

He bound her wrists behind her back.

A click sounded. Like a door latching.

A few minutes later, Elise heard more clicks and then an engine started. Slowly, the vehicle rolled down a gravel road.

Whoever had abducted her must have parked on a side road, somewhere no one would see his vehicle.

But the bigger question was: where would he take her?

As the car continued to move down the road, all Elise could think about was the people she loved.

Daniel's face plowed into her memories. He would have never wanted this for her. His whole life, he'd tried to protect her. He'd tried to protect his country. And, in return, someone had betrayed him and made him look like a traitor.

Her stomach turned at the thought.

Her thoughts shifted to Colton next. She didn't think it possible that she'd ever fall in love again. And it wasn't that she was in love with Colton, but Elise could feel something growing inside her. Something sweet and warm. Something she didn't want to let go of.

Elise had failed Daniel. But she vowed she'd never be that person again. She had to fight for the people she believed in.

She felt around the back of the vehicle. It was clean, absent of any stray leaves or specks of wood or anything else one might feel in the back of an often-used vehicle. Could the car be a rental?

Maybe.

But that also meant there was nothing back here, nothing to protect herself with.

What did they do in some of those TV shows? The victim felt around until she found a latch that would open the trunk. Or she kicked out the brake light so she could see where she was.

The black bag made it hard to move, do much of anything.

Instead, Elise mentally tried to keep track of where they were. She hadn't felt the driver turn anywhere. Did that mean they were headed down the main stretch of highway that went north and south on the island? It made the most sense.

What was at the other end? If she remembered correctly, the ferry docks were down there as well as an old harbor. The lighthouse wasn't too far from that area either.

What would this man do with her at any of those places? Certainly, the ferry wasn't operating at this hour.

Keep thinking, Elise. Keep thinking.

Who was the person who'd grabbed her? He was strong. He didn't even breathe hard as he carried her. He felt like nothing but solid muscles beneath her.

Benjamin?

No, why would he even pop into her head. Benjamin wasn't a bad guy, despite the conflict between him and the rest of the team. He wouldn't do that.

Who else?

The man who'd come into The Crazy Chefette fluttered through her mind also. What was his name? Leonardo?

He was obviously strong and capable, and he just happened to be on the island right now. Could it have been him?

She couldn't rule him out.

Henry? She didn't think so. Her gut told her the man had been telling the truth.

Maybe it was someone she hadn't put her eyes on yet—a member of the Savages who blended in.

But nothing made sense still.

Elise had to figure this out. Her life depended on it.

CHAPTER THIRTY-FOUR

"HOW MUCH FARTHER AWAY IS THE bomb-sniffing dog?" Colton peered out the window, trying to get a good look at the bomb. But the angle was bad, and it was dark outside.

He only knew he couldn't do anything to risk setting the device off. They'd be no good to Elise if they were dead.

"Dane is trying to get a friend to bring him over on a boat right now," Cassidy said. "But I'm going to say he's at least an hour away. My guys are on their way here also. The bad news is that they don't have much bomb training."

"We don't have an hour." Colton felt his hands fist at his side.

"Since we're all stuck here," Ty started. "How about

we look at this evidence one more time? If we can figure out who this implicates, then we can figure out who grabbed Elise."

Reluctantly, Colton nodded. It was a good idea. It would keep their minds occupied until the bomb was disarmed. Right now, he felt like he was going crazy.

He pulled printouts of the evidence from a folder he'd left in the office and brought them to the kitchen table.

Cassidy picked up one with the code on it. "Is there some kind of cypher for this?"

"If there is, we haven't figured it out yet. The woman who was helping us died in a car accident."

"Lots of accidents and tragedies surrounding this, aren't there?" Cassidy frowned.

"You can say that again," Colton said. "I've had no luck figuring it out myself. None of us have."

"Let me take a look at this. I actually took a class on it back when I was in . . ." Cassidy's voice trailed off, and she shook her head. "Back when I did my police training."

"That will work. Ty, could you examine these pictures? I'm going to try to get Tara Campbell's boyfriend on the phone."

"You know it's 2:30 in the morning, don't you?" Ty asked.

"I do. But this is life or death. It can't wait."

While everyone else got to work, Colton went into

the office and used the secure line there to dial Joseph Monsoon's number. A sleepy and slightly annoyed voice answered on the third ring.

"This better be important."

"Someone is going to die if you don't answer my questions." Colton prayed the man wouldn't hang up.

"Who is this?" Joseph asked.

"I'm a former Navy SEAL, and I believe that your girlfriend was going to expose somebody who was working with the Savages. I believe she was framed, along with one of my friends. If I don't find answers soon, I have another friend who will die. You've got to help me."

Silence stretched for a moment until Joseph finally said, "I can't talk over the phone. I can't risk it."

"This is a secure line. No one's going to hear what we have to say."

Joseph didn't say anything for a moment. Finally, he said, "What do you need to know?"

ELISE DIDN'T KNOW what was going on. The car ride felt like it took forever, but she knew the island wasn't that big. She hadn't felt them turn yet. The tires continued to roll over the road, but there was nothing to give her a clue as to where they were.

She managed to turn over so her hands faced the

back of the trunk. She felt around but couldn't find the release lever.

There had to be something else she could do.

Maybe there was a way to get this black bag from her head. If she rubbed her head against the carpet maybe she could get traction and pull it off. If only she had a little more room . . . but she didn't. She needed to make the best of what she had.

Elise rubbed her head against the carpet. But, instead of removing the bag around her head, she only felt her cheek burning from the friction.

That wasn't going to work.

Find something sharp to cut the tape from around your hands.

Just as she began to feel for something that might work, the car came to a stop.

Her breath caught.

Where were they? What was this man going to do with her now that they were here?

Stark fear rushed through her.

She wouldn't give up the information. It didn't matter what they did to her. But Elise didn't look forward to whatever lay ahead. Part of her just wanted to curl into a ball and pretend like none of this was happening.

But that wasn't an option. All of this had been set in motion, and now she needed to see it to completion.

She only hoped that completion didn't mean her death.

CHAPTER THIRTY-FIVE

"TARA FELT like she was being targeted by someone on the inside," Joseph said.

"On the inside of what?" Colton crossed his arms as he waited for the man's answer.

"Inside the government. She felt somebody on her team was giving up secrets and information, and she was determined to figure out who."

Colton's spine tightened. "Did she ever mention any names?"

"The only name I ever heard her mention was Daniel Oliver's."

"She thought Daniel was a traitor?" Colton tensed as he heard the words leave his mouth.

"I didn't say Tara thought he was a traitor. In fact, I think he was one of the only people that she trusted."

That made more sense. Colton released his breath.

"Did she say anything about her work in the days leading up to her death?"

"She seemed distracted. I could tell whatever she was working on had gotten her down."

"Is there anything else that you know that might help us figure out who is behind this?"

"This is all I know. When she was stationed overseas, she saw the leader of the Savages meeting with an American. It was dark, and she couldn't see much. Only that he was young. Strong. He had dark hair."

Benjamin? Could it have been his teammate? He'd been in Virginia Beach the night Elise was attacked. He had the skills. The know-how.

Colton really didn't want to believe that, though.

Keep thinking, Colton.

Based on that description, Colton could rule out Commander Larson and Secretary Stabler.

Who else did that leave?

"Tara was trying to figure out who that person was," Joseph continued. "But as soon as she voiced concern, she began feeling like someone was watching her. I know she and Daniel went to some fundraiser together. They heard a meeting was going to take place there. Before they could figure out who the traitor was, the fire alarm went off and everyone was cleared from the room. They weren't able to get the answers they needed."

"That's too bad." Disappointment pressed on him.

"But she did find a drop site a few days later."

Colton's back straightened. "You mean, like the kind in spy movies?"

"Just like that. There was a paper with some kind of code inside. She couldn't crack it."

Colton sucked in a breath. The code. That's where it had come from.

"Thanks for your help," he told Joseph.

Just as Colton ended the call, someone called him back into the living area.

"I think I might know what this code is," Cassidy said. "And, if I'm right, I know what the first few words are."

ELISE BLINKED, trying to gather a sense of her surroundings. But the black bag covering her eyes didn't allow her to see anything. No light escaped through the material.

A strong hand grabbed her and jerked her from the trunk. The man set her on her feet, took her arm, and yanked her behind him.

Flashbacks of that night at her house filled her mind—when the man had dragged her into her kitchen so quickly that her legs could hardly keep up.

This was the same man, wasn't it? Was there ever any doubt?

She continued to stumble forward. It felt like asphalt beneath her shoes. Occasionally, she felt a stray rock.

The scent of the sea blew in with the breeze. They were close to water. Elise sniffed. And fish. It smelled fishy here.

They were at the docks, weren't they? Elise wasn't sure if it was the ferry dock or the harbor area, but she would guess it was one of them.

She almost wished that the man would talk. That she could hear his voice again and try to identify him that way. But he remained quiet, only grunting on occasion.

Her arm already ached from where his fingers dug into her flesh.

Despair tried to bite at her, but she held it back. She couldn't give in to it. If she did, it could cost her life.

They stopped. But the man didn't release his grip on her. She heard jangling.

Keys?

A moment later, a loud creak cut through the air, and the man shoved her. She tumbled forward, hitting her knees on something that felt like cement.

"I'll be right back," the man muttered.

The next instant, the door slammed again.

Despair came back, stronger this time. The feeling tried to claim Elise's soul, her thoughts, her heart.

And, with every second that passed, it was becoming harder to fight it.

"WHAT DOES THE CODE SAY?" Colton moved closer to Cassidy so he could see. She sat at the kitchen table, bent over the code with a paper and pencil beside her.

"I'm not 100 percent sure, but this looks like a code that my—that somebody I used to be close to, I mean—used on occasion for his computer programs. There were corporate spies within the business and that's why the code was developed. It's just a combination of letters and numbers, but the pattern doesn't repeat in a logical way. But once you have everything lined up . . ."

"I'm not really concerned what the code is," Colton said. "I trust you. I really need to know what it says."

"I only had time to do the first few lines, but they are, 'Our plan is coming together. The players are in place.'"

Whatever that meant, it wasn't good.

"Take a look at this." Ty held up the picture that Daniel had taken. "I've been playing with various filters on this, trying to clarify a few of these pictures. If you look at this reflection here, who does that look like in the mirror?"

Colton squinted and looked closer. "It almost looks like...Leonardo."

"Bingo." Ty's gaze met his. "I thought it was weird that he just happened to show up at the island just now."

"So did I," Colton said. "And as soon as we're able to get out of this house, I think we need to pay him a visit."

Just as he said the words, he heard somebody pull up. Colton glanced out the window and saw . . . Benjamin standing there.

He still didn't look happy, but he was here.

"Griff called me," he said. "I think I might be able to help."

CHAPTER THIRTY-SIX

DANIEL WOULD WANT her to be happy.

That was the conclusion that Elise had drawn after sitting in the cold, dank room for the past several minutes. She didn't know how much time had passed. On one hand, it felt like hours and, on the other, only seconds.

She knew the man would be back soon.

What would Daniel do in this situation? Elise had already stood and tried to feel her way around the place, but she'd had no luck. It didn't help that her hands were bound.

For starters, Daniel probably wouldn't have found himself in this situation. But if he was here, he would be on the defensive.

Elise knew the statistics. She knew that if a person got into the car with a criminal, the victim was less likely to ever be seen again. Elise *had* gotten into the vehicle with somebody, and now she was here.

She had no idea what this man was planning to do with her, but Elise was certain he'd use pain as a technique to get information from her.

She squeezed her eyes shut, but she couldn't tell any difference between having her eyes opened or closed. It was too dark in here, and she had this bag over her head.

Daniel would tell her to keep a cool head. Up until the past couple months before he died, he had always been calm and in control. So what had he discovered during those last two months that had shaken him up so much he wasn't even acting like himself?

And how had he discovered this information?

It was obviously important to him if he had gone through all the trouble to hide it. Elise had a feeling that he had planned on using it when he returned from that last mission. He just never got a chance.

Now it was time for Elise to pick up where he'd left off. She was going to figure out what Daniel had discovered, and she was going to do something about it.

But first she had to get out of her current situation.

Just as a thought entered her head, she heard the door open and felt a whoosh of cool air come into the room. She braced herself for whatever was about to happen next.

OVER A SPAN of the ten minutes, Benjamin had discovered three bombs. He disarmed the one at the cottage first.

As soon as the door opened, Colton stepped outside. Though he wanted to dash to his vehicle, he stopped for long enough to meet Benjamin's gaze.

"Thank you," he muttered.

Benjamin nodded but said nothing else.

Colton would talk to him later. For now, he rushed to his car.

Before he pulled away, Dez appeared at his window.

"You got out already?" Colton rushed.

"Once Benjamin figured out how to disarm the first bomb, the second one went quickly."

"Hop in."

Dez climbed into the passenger side seat, and Colton took off. He knew exactly where he needed to head—to the inn where Leonardo was staying.

It was still early. Only 4:30 AM. But he would wake people up if that was what he had to do to get some answers.

He threw his car in Park and pounded up the front steps to the inn. He tried the front door, but it was locked. Instead, he rang the bell. Five minutes later, a sleepy-eyed woman came to the door with her robe pulled around her.

"Where's the fire?" she asked, wrapping her arms across her chest.

"We need to talk to a guest of yours. His name is Leonardo."

As soon as he said the man's name, a smile crossed the woman's lips. Colton had seen that look before. This lady obviously thought that Leonardo was good-looking.

"He's in room 2B. But I can't let you go—"

Before she could finish the sentence, they pushed past her and started up the steps. As soon as they reached his door, Colton pounded on it. Leonardo answered, looking more annoyed than he did tired.

"What do you think you're doing here?" Leonardo stared at them with something close to vengeance in his eyes.

The fact that he was at the inn right now seemed a good indicator that he hadn't taken Elise. But what if he was working with someone?

"Where is she?" Colton grabbed Leonardo by his shirt and pushed him back until he hit the wall.

"I don't know what you're talking about. Where is who?" His eyes bulged as he stared at Colton.

"Where is Elise?"

"Daniel's girl?" His voice rose an octave. "I don't know where she is. Why would I?"

"Because this trouble didn't start until you came to the island." Dez stepped up beside Colton and stared Leonardo down. "We need to find her. She's in danger."

"Well, I haven't seen her."

"So you're saying you don't have anything to do with what's been going on here?" Dez clarified.

"I have no idea what you're talking about. When I told you I came here to try to get a job, I was telling the truth." Sweat spread across his skin.

"What about this picture?" Colton pulled it from his pocket and held it up.

Leonardo took it from him and squinted as he examined it further. "Where did you get this?"

"It's not important," Colton said.

He stared at it another moment before shrugging. "I don't know. It's too fuzzy. I'm not really sure where it was taken."

"Look closer." Colton's voice came out as a growl.

Leonardo scowled at him for a moment before looking back at the photo. He let out a sigh before saying, "That almost looks like it was taken at the benefit gala for Sarah's Promise."

Sarah's Promise helped build schools for underprivileged communities overseas. Colton had only heard about the organization. Since it was started by the wife of a high-ranking official, many in the military supported it.

"You were there?" Colton asked.

Leonardo swallowed hard before nodding. "As a matter of fact, I was."

"Do you remember anything strange about that evening?" Dez pressed.

"I can't say I do. Then, again, that was more than a year ago. It didn't seem all that important at the time."

"Do you know who any of these other people in the pictures are?" Colton held up the photos again.

"As a matter of fact, I do. That's Commander Larson. Secretary Stabler. Brian Starks. He's one of the commander's assistants."

Colton and Dez exchanged a look.

"Do you know anything about Brian Starks?" Dez asked.

"I can't say I do. Never really had a chance to talk to the man that much. But he seemed very knowledgeable and helpful every time I did."

"If there's anything you know that might help us find Elise or figure out who's behind this, you need to tell us," Colton said.

Something flickered in Leonardo's gaze, but he said nothing.

"What is it?" Colton demanded, stepping closer to Leonardo.

"It's probably nothing." Leonardo raised his hand, as if pleading with Colton to stay back.

"Tell us," Dez said. "We'll take anything at this point."

"Benjamin was there."

Just then, Colton's phone rang. It was Cassidy.

"Find anything new?" he answered.

"I have a few more words of this code. It says, 'Our plan is coming together. The players are in place. This will cripple the US. We just need to take out the key people first.'"

The Savages had moved onto US soil. There was no doubt about that.

"One other thing," Cassidy said. "I just got a call. A shrimp trawler was hijacked. The crew was set out on life rafts. The Coast Guard just picked them up."

"A shrimp trawler?" Colton said. "I'm going to need a boat."

"I can get you one of those. And I just sent my crew to the harbor."

CHAPTER THIRTY-SEVEN

THE MAN DRAGGED Elise from the room where she had been stashed. The cold rushed at her again. They were outside, she realized. Near the water. Where the wind was always several degrees chillier.

The unknown sent a shot of terror through her. She didn't know where she was, though she assumed it was a harbor. She didn't know what the man looked like. Nor did she know where he was taking her or what he was planning to do with her here. The deprivation of her senses had proven to only make her fear grow deeper.

Fear, you will not win. You had your moment. Now it's time for courage to step up to the plate.

But Elise would be lying if she didn't acknowledge that she had a bad feeling about all of this.

Had Colton discovered that she was missing yet?

Was he looking for her? And the even bigger question: would he find her?

"Step up," the man ordered.

Before she could follow his directions, the man shoved her. Her foot caught on something in front of her, and she tumbled forward again. This time, there was nothing on the other side. She fell until her body hit something with a thud.

Pain spread through her. Wherever she'd landed, it was cold. And wet. And . . . it moved back and forth. It swayed, for that matter.

He'd taken her to a boat, she realized.

Elise wished she could get up, that she could try to fight this. She heard the man moving around. Her captor had obviously jumped on board with her. She didn't know what he was doing, but she imagined he was preparing to launch the boat. A few minutes later, she heard an engine and felt movement.

They were headed out to sea, she realized.

Elise didn't think it was possible for her fear to grow any deeper, but it did. Out there, there would be nowhere to run.

The ocean was deadly and unrelenting.

If this man didn't kill her, then the Atlantic would.

IT TOOK twenty minutes for Cassidy to secure a boat.

Colton felt certain the man who'd abducted Elise had taken her out on the water. The man didn't plan on staying on this island with Elise. It would be too risky.

If Leonardo wasn't behind this, then who was? Could it be Brian Starks? He was a possibility. The man was almost a wallflower. But he was always there. Always listening. It was the perfect job for someone who wanted to spy for the enemy.

The thing Colton couldn't understand was why he'd never seen this man on the island. Certainly, he would have recognized him.

As they headed out on the water, Colton's anxiety grew. The way the wind blew . . . the way the waves kicked up . . . there was a storm stirring. They didn't have any time to waste.

Dez put his phone to his ear and then looked back at Colton. "A small craft warning has been issued."

"Then let's move faster."

Colton just prayed they got to Elise in time.

CHAPTER THIRTY-EIGHT

FINALLY, the roar of the engine died down. Elise heard footsteps coming toward her as she lay on the floor, unable to move. A moment later, the man yanked her to her feet and shoved her into some sort of seat.

Elise held her breath, waiting for whatever was coming next. Was the man holding a gun to her? Or knife?

She had no idea.

Next thing she knew, the bag around her head was snatched off.

Elise blinked, trying to get her surroundings into focus.

She was definitely on a boat out in the ocean. The darkness around her . . . it nearly swallowed them. It was impossible to see where the sky ended and the ocean began.

But it was the man in front of her that took her breath away.

"Jason?" she muttered. "But..."

He'd transformed from the so-called homeless man into somebody much more determined and driven. His eyes even took on a new light—the light of someone calculated and deadly.

He reached up and tugged at his hairline. As he pulled it back, he revealed a wig.

She blinked again. Elise had seen this man before. His dark long hair had been so overwhelming that it obstructed his features. But now that she looked closer ... was he in one of those pictures that Daniel had stowed away? She couldn't be certain. There was something else...

"Do you know who I am yet?" A gleam sparkled in his eyes.

"I've seen you before."

He grinned, looking a little too satisfied. "Yes, you have."

Elise sucked in a breath as realization washed over her. "You were the man who was driving the limo that day I met with the commander."

"Give the girl a diploma," he said with a chuckle. "You finally put the pieces together."

"You were the one behind this the whole time?" As she said the words, a wave crashed into them and the boat rocked. Water sprayed over the deck, chilling her to the bone.

No one should be out in this water tonight. No one.

"My name *is* Jason. Jason Perkins. Proud member of the US Navy at your service."

"Why are you doing this?" Elise tugged at the binds around her wrists. The moisture seemed to loosen them. If only she could slide her hands out . . .

"I'm just following orders."

"Orders from who?"

"The Savages, of course." He smiled.

"The Savages sent you after me? Why would a group like that be so focused on me?"

"I think we both know the answer to that question. I need those papers and the other evidence that you found."

She raised her chin. "I don't have them with me."

"Where are they."

"I can't tell you that."

He stepped closer. "Oh, you're going to tell me that information."

As a moment of fear swept over her, Elise considered backing off. "I can't do that."

He reached for her throat and pressed until the air no longer went into her lungs. Panic rushed through her.

"Are you sure about that?" he growled.

He released his grip on her long enough for her to rasp, "You might as well go ahead and kill me."

"Oh, I'm going to do that. But I need that information first."

More water slapped over the edges of the boat, and a wave jostled them, nearly sending them toppling to the other side of the boat.

Please, Lord . . . help us.

"Why did you bring me out here?" she asked.

"So I could show you exactly how your husband died. In fact, I'm going to do more than show you how he died. You're going to experience it for yourself."

Anger displaced some of her fear. Elise narrowed her eyes and stared at Jason. "You're sick."

"I kind of like it this way." He grinned again.

"You won't get away with this." She tugged at her binds again. Her wrist finally slipped.

The duct tape came off, and her hands were free. She wasn't sure how much good that would do her now, though. Jason could easily overpower her.

"Of course I will. Who else is out here who is going to stop me?"

Another chill rushed through her at his words. "Blackout is going to find you."

"Blackout is going to die when I accidentally set off one of those bombs I left around the house."

"They're smarter than that. They're going to find

the bombs, and they're going to figure out a way to find me."

"I like your optimism, but that's not the way it's going to work out." Jason's hand squeezed her throat again. "Now, do you want to rethink telling me that information?"

"THERE IT IS!" Colton yelled.

He spotted the shrimp trawler in the distance and cut the lights on his boat. He slowed, trying not to alert anyone onboard that he was coming. The darkness would be his friend right now—but these waves wouldn't.

A storm stirred in the distance.

His phone rang, and he saw a new message from Griff. His friend had managed to enlarge that photo. Colton handed the steering to Dez and clicked on the picture.

In the corner of the photo, he spotted a new face in the corner—barely reflected in the mirror.

"What is it?" Dez asked.

Colton sucked in a breath as realization washed over him. "That's Jason, the homeless guy here on the island."

"What's he doing at a charity event like that?" Dez said. "Weren't tickets hundreds of dollars?"

"He's obviously not homeless. That must have just been a cover." Colton's stomach clenched at the thought.

He called Griff, needing more information.

"I had a friend of mine run his photo through the system," Griff said. "Our homeless guy is actually Jason Perkins. He was a combat driver in the Navy, but his vehicle hit an IED. He spent months in recovery. When he was finally released, he had a career change and became a different kind of driver—he became part of Secretary Stabler's entourage. His main task is acting as chauffeur."

Colton didn't like the sound of any of this. "Any idea how he got involved with the Savages?"

"I'm still researching it. But I heard when he was stationed overseas, he became friendly with the locals. My guess is that's how he got involved. He could have begun sympathizing with them. Maybe his goal all along was to get in a position with someone high-ranking so he could get inside information."

"Keep researching. Good job."

"Do you think someone sent him here to do the job? And, if they did, was it the Savages or someone inside the command?"

Colton didn't even want to think about the possibility. Right now, he just needed to concentrate on finding Elise and making sure that she was safe. As long as Colton knew she would be okay, then hope remained that maybe they could talk things through. That maybe he could somehow convince Elise that he'd only been trying to protect her. Maybe she would forgive him.

He called Cassidy and gave her their coordinates. They would need all the help they could get. Colton didn't know if they were going up against one guy or many. He only knew he didn't want to be ambushed again.

As they got closer to the trawler, they cut the engine and drifted the rest of the way. Just as they got on the backside of the boat, a male voice rang out.

"This is what Daniel felt like before he died," the deep voice crowed.

"You're sick," someone said. Elise.

As Colton's eyes continued to adjust to the darkness, he saw Elise on the bow. Jason loomed in front of her.

Colton nodded at Dez before boarding the boat. Using all the stealth within him, he crept closer to the scene. Jason didn't seem to hear him. That was a good sign.

But as Colton got closer to her, the fear in Elise's eyes became clear.

He had to stop this now.

CHAPTER THIRTY-NINE

JASON STEPPED AWAY FROM HER, and Elise sucked in deep breaths of air. She watched as he reached down and pulled out... a gun.

Not just any gun.

An automatic machine gun.

That weapon could take out someone long-range without a problem. And Jason stood only a few feet away from her.

This nightmare was far from over.

Elise looked below and saw the dark water there. The weather had been growing worse, and the waves were becoming larger by the moment. As the wind swept over the boat, Elise grabbed the railing so she wouldn't lose her balance.

Her throat went dry at the sight of that water. It

could be her grave. There was no way she would survive out here for very long. No one could.

Was this what Daniel felt? Had he been afraid? Elise had a hard time seeing it. He'd always seemed so valiant, so fearless.

"You got your hands free," Jason muttered. "But that's not going to help you now."

Elise ignored him, tried to push away the fear he tried to stir inside her. "How did you know about the items I found?"

"Easy. I heard you talking to the commander."

That's what she assumed. "Then you started following me?"

"I did. This would've been so much easier if you had just given me that information that day I went to your house."

Anger zinged through her blood as she remembered her house fire. "You didn't have to kill Bernie."

"I wouldn't have if he hadn't gotten in my way."

Acid burned in her stomach. This man was disgusting. Absolutely disgusting. "Then you had to pull Henry into this as well."

"The plan was brilliant, and it messed with your mind," Jason said. "Win-win. You've got to know that we will do whatever it takes to get our way."

"Why did you even target him?" she asked.

"He was my Uber driver. He talked about how much he loved his wife. Even had a picture of her on his dashboard. I got his license plate number and tracked down his address. He was the perfect target. He practically handed himself to me."

"So I see. Innocent lives mean nothing to you."

"There's no such thing as an innocent life." Jason chuckled as if the idea was entertaining.

"How many of you are there here?" Buy time, Elise. Just buy time.

His laughter faded, and that intense look returned to his eyes. "I can't answer that question. Now, enough talking."

Elise could hardly stand to think about it. There was so much evil and corruption out there. Sometimes it felt useless to even fight it. But what other choice did she have?

"Now tell me where the information is." Jason raised his gun again.

Fear trembled through her again. "I told you, I can't do that. What's it going to matter? If I'm dead, no one's going to find it anyway."

"We can't know that. That's why we need it." He stepped closer and pressed the gun into her side until she gasped.

"You're out of luck then." The waves rose and fell again, reminding her of a rollercoaster—a terrifying rollercoaster. More water splashed aboard. If the boat tossed too much, Jason could accidentally pull the trigger.

"Then after this, I'll just have to kill off your friends one by one until they give me the copies you gave them."

Elise felt her face go paler. "Leave them out of this."

"Too late. You pulled them into this."

Just as Jason said the words, she spotted movement behind him. Was she seeing things?

But she knew she wasn't.

Colton. That was Colton. He was on the boat.

Her heart soared. Maybe there was hope.

But as she glanced at the gun again, her hope began to plummet. One pull of Jason's finger and her life would be over . . . just like Daniel's had been.

COLTON HAD to make his move. It was now or never. As he saw the man raise his gun back up toward Elise's head, he knew that time was running out. He glanced on the other side of the boat and spotted Dez there.

Between the two of them, they could take Jason out. Colton hadn't seen anybody else on the boat. Jason had clearly anticipated an easy mission.

"This is your last chance," Jason said. "Tell me what I need to know."

"I can't do that," Elise said.

"Okay, but I feel like it's only fair to warn you that this water is so cold that it will kill you in less than five minutes. That's if the sharks don't get you first or if the currents don't pull you out."

Elise visibly shuddered. But she said nothing.

"Have it your way," Jason said.

Before he could pull the trigger, Colton darted from his hiding place and tackled him. Their bodies collided, and they hit the deck. As they did, Jason's gun fell to the ground—but not before firing.

Colton gasped and looked up. Elise tumbled over the railing. Had she been hit?

Colton's heart leapt into his throat. "No!"

Dez grabbed Jason's arms, securing him in place. "I've got him. Go get Elise."

Without thinking about it anymore, Colton ran to the edge of the boat. He reached the railing just in time to see Elise go under.

He dove in after her, determined that he wasn't going to lose her now.

CHAPTER FORTY

ELISE FELT the cold water hit her, and the air left her lungs. She had never felt such cold, such overwhelming cold. It seeped into every part of her body until she felt like she could no longer move.

Another wave came and covered her head. Elise managed to pop back up. To take a breath. Her limbs weren't cooperating, and moving was a struggle.

But she had to try.

Another wave pulled her under again, farther and deeper this time.

Elise sputtered as she came up. Water filled her nose, her mouth.

She wouldn't last long out here. Not in these conditions.

Daniel . . . was this how he'd felt? Or had his death been quick?

Strong arms wrapped around her. As she surfaced from the water again, she heard someone say, "I've got you."

Colton. Colton had come after her.

He swam with her toward the shrimp trawler in the distance. As they got closer, Dez reached down and pulled her onto the boat. She collapsed there, sputtering and coughing water from her lungs. Uncontrollable shivers claimed her entire body.

Colton surfaced a moment later. With Dez's help, he climbed aboard. Trembles overwhelmed his body, but all of his focus seemed to be on her.

He bent down next to her. "Were you shot?"

Elise did a quick inventory, her thoughts murky and unclear. "No . . . I don't think so."

He closed his eyes and bent toward her. "Thank goodness."

Just as the words left his lips, lights shone in the distance.

Backup was here, Elise realized. Maybe this was finally over.

CHAPTER FORTY-ONE

AN HOUR LATER, they were all back on the shore and Jason had been taken into custody.

Elise was tucked safely into the back of Cassidy's police cruiser. A paramedic checked her vitals, while Cassidy took her statement.

Thank goodness, the Coast Guard had shown up when it did. Just one slip in the timing of everything, and they might not all be here right now.

As a familiar face appeared in the distance, Colton straightened his back.

It was time to make things right.

Colton strode across the parking area of the docks. The sun was beginning to rise, scattering its light around him. It promised a new day, a new start.

Colton paused in front of Benjamin and swallowed his pride. "Thank you for your help earlier."

"It's no problem." But Benjamin's words still sounded hard.

"I'm sorry I doubted you."

Benjamin shrugged, his shoulders stiff. "I know you don't know me as well as you know the other guys . . . but if you gave me a chance, maybe you would see I'm not that bad."

"You're right. And I'm sorry. I think we were all looking for someone to blame. I should have never set my sights on you."

Benjamin stared at him another moment before nodding. "It's okay."

Colton felt his muscles loosen.

Benjamin reached for his hand, and their grips locked before they gave each other a man hug.

If Benjamin could forgive Colton, then maybe Colton should forgive himself.

Jason had been the one who'd sold them out. He'd heard everything that had been planned, and he'd told the Savages about the SEAL team coming to take out their leader. The man had positioned himself to obtain information and then use it against the US. His plan had been clever.

Thank goodness, he was behind bars now.

He saw Cassidy climb from the police car and stride toward them. Colton met her halfway.

"Everything good?"

"She's asking for you."

Colton felt a surprising wave of anxiety. He didn't know which way this conversation would go. But more than anything, he needed to see Elise right now and know that she was okay.

ELISE HAD blankets wrapped around her as she sat in a police car with the heat blasting.

The warmth had never felt so good.

She'd been so certain she was going to die out there. So certain.

But as she watched the sun rise in the distance, she lifted up thanks that she'd been given another chance. Death had been so close she'd practically been able to reach out and touch it.

Colton slipped into the back of the car beside her, a hot cup of coffee in each hand. They'd both changed into something dry—Cassidy had brought some spare clothes with her to the scene.

"Lisa just dropped this by." Colton handed her a cardboard cup.

"That was nice of her. Thank you." She glanced at Colton, her heart filling with gratitude and appreciation. But there was more than that. The affection she felt for Colton surprised even her.

Being with him this week had reignited something in her, a spark she never thought she'd feel again.

She offered him part of her blanket. "You need to stay warm also."

"I'll be okay. It's you I'm worried about."

She scooted closer and draped part of it over his legs anyway. "I'm alive. I can't ask for much more."

Their gazes caught, and a million unspoken conversations passed between them. There was so much Elise needed to say. That she wanted to hear. Whatever happened next could determine their future.

"Elise—" Colton started.

"It's okay," Elise said quickly. "I know why you couldn't tell me."

His gaze softened, his relief visible. "I wanted to. I really did."

She reached beneath the blanket and squeezed his hand. "I know. When Jason grabbed me, my priorities suddenly became very clear. Facing death can do that to a person. I knew beyond a doubt that I wanted you in my future."

Colton's features softened as he leaned toward her. "Hearing that makes me happy. Very happy."

A smile tugged at Elise's lips. "I'm glad."

He reached for her, and his hand splayed at her neck, her jaw. Colton closed the space between them and his lips met hers. The kiss only lasted a minute before Colton put an arm around Elise and folded her into his arms.

She rested her head against his chest and imagined a future where she could do this every day.

Nothing sounded better.

CHAPTER FORTY-TWO

TWENTY-FOUR HOURS LATER, when Colton woke up after a full night's rest, he felt lighter than he had in a year.

Jason Perkins was in custody.

Henry's wife, Alice, had been located and was being checked at a hospital up in Nags Head.

Elise was safe.

He and Benjamin had made amends.

Even better—Colton and Elise were going to have breakfast this morning at The Crazy Chefette. Just the two of them.

He couldn't wait.

Thirty minutes later, they were seated across from each other at the restaurant.

Though an entire day had passed since Jason's arrest, everything felt like a blur. Yesterday had been spent answering questions from numerous law enforcement agencies. Commander Stabler himself had called, and they'd given him a rundown on things. He'd thanked Colton and the team for their service and promised that NCIS would take matters from here.

Colton and Elise had grabbed snippets of time together. But as soon as they'd gotten back to the cottage, they'd both crashed.

Finally, they had some time alone.

After ordering, Colton looked across the table at Elise. At lovely, lovely Elise. Even with that wound on her forehead and her stiff motions from being manhandled by Jason, she was still a sight to behold. The most beautiful woman he'd ever set eyes on, hands down.

"So, are you ready to tell me where you hid the evidence?" He leaned toward her from across the table.

A smile tugged at her lips. "If you must know, it's in the freezer in the workroom at my office."

He raised his eyebrows. "What?"

She offered a half shrug. "It was a trick Daniel taught me. I put all of the information into a Ziplock bag. Then I scooped out half a gallon of chocolate mint ice cream, hid the bag in the middle of the container, and refroze the ice cream."

Clever but . . . "How did you know no one would eat it?"

"Easy. I left a note on it saying no one should touch it and that I'd eaten out of it right before I got the flu."

He chuckled as he pictured it. "Smart thinking."

"NCIS was able to retrieve it, so I guess it worked."

Cassidy stepped into the restaurant and wandered over to their table.

"How are you two today?" she asked.

"We're doing great," Elise said. "Thanks, in part, to you."

"It wasn't just me. We're all a team around here."

"You off to another protest?" Colton asked.

"Actually . . ." Cassidy shifted. "Some of the homeowners filed a lawsuit against the developer, and the project has been put on hold. So no more protests for a while."

"That's good news, at least, right?" Elise said.

"I'm not complaining." Cassidy winked. "I'll let you guys get back to your talk. Good to see you two out and about."

As Cassidy left, Elise leaned back and stared out the window a moment. Her thoughts were obviously churning. "What I still can't figure out is how that picture of Daniel was taken at the bank. I understand that someone could have set up that account in his name but . . ."

"My guess is that Jason sent Daniel to the bank and told him the commander had ordered it. When Daniel was there, he was probably just picking up some forms or something innocent. But that picture was snapped just at the right time. All of that was so Daniel would look like one of the bad guys. Jason knew Tara and Daniel were closing in. That's why he sold them out."

"Daniel was close to blowing all of this open." Elise took a cup of coffee the waitress brought, thanked her, and then turned back to Colton.

"That's why he was such a threat. Jason will get his trial. Maybe the authorities will even get some information out of him in the process. You did a good job, Elise."

"Thank you." Elise rewarded him with a smile.

"What now?" His smile slipped as he waited for her answer. He'd been thinking about it all day yesterday. Did this mean Elise would return to her life in Virginia Beach? If so, what did that mean for them?

"Ty talked to me yesterday about possibly helping out with Hope House."

Colton's breath caught. "And what do you think?"

"The pay's not great, but my coworkers would be awesome." She grinned at him. "What do you think?"

He reached across the table and took her hand into his. "I think . . . you should do whatever you want. But I would love to have you here."

"That's good to hear, because I accepted the position."

A grin spread across his face. "That just made my whole year."

"I was hoping it might. I'm really looking forward to the change."

"Me too."

They exchanged a smile, and Colton knew that this breakfast together would be the first of many.

And he couldn't wait to see what the future held.

DEEP HARBOR: LANTERN BEACH BLACKOUT, BOOK 2

A JOB AS EASY AS SUNDAY MORNING

Guilt over past mistakes haunt former Navy SEAL Dez

Rodriguez. When he's asked to guard a pop star during a music festival on Lantern Beach, he's all set for what he hopes is a breezy assignment.

UNTIL HE MEETS BREE JORDAN
Bree hasn't found fame to be nearly as fulfilling as she dreamed. Instead, she's more like a carefully crafted character living out a pre-scripted story. When a stalker's threats become deadly, her life—and career—are turned upside down.

DANGER RISES UP THE CHARTS
From the start, Bree sees her temporary bodyguard as a player, and Dez sees Bree as a spoiled rich girl. But when they're thrown together in a fight for survival, both must learn to trust. Can Dez protect Bree—and his carefully guarded heart? Or will their safe harbor ultimately become their death trap?

ALSO BY CHRISTY BARRITT:

OTHER BOOKS IN THE LANTERN
BEACH SERIES:

LANTERN BEACH MYSTERIES

Hidden Currents

You can take the detective out of the investigation, but you can't take the investigator out of the detective. A notorious gang puts a bounty on Detective Cady Matthews's head after she takes down their leader, leaving her no choice but to hide until she can testify at trial. But her temporary home across the country on a remote North Carolina island isn't as peaceful as she initially thinks. Living under the new identity of Cassidy Livingston, she struggles to keep her investigative skills tucked away, especially after a body washes ashore. When local police bungle the murder investigation, she can't resist stepping in. But Cassidy is supposed to be keeping a low profile. One wrong move could lead to both her discovery and her demise. Can she bring justice to the island . . . or will the hidden currents surrounding her pull her under for good?

Flood Watch

The tide is high, and so is the danger on Lantern Beach. Still in hiding after infiltrating a dangerous gang, Cassidy Livingston just has to make it a few more months before she can testify at trial and resume her old life. But trouble keeps finding her, and Cassidy is pulled into a local investigation after a man mysteriously disappears from the island she now calls home. A recurring nightmare from her time undercover only muddies things, as does a visit from the parents of her handsome ex-Navy SEAL neighbor. When a friend's life is threatened, Cassidy must make choices that put her on the verge of blowing her cover. With a flood watch on her emotions and her life in a tangle, will Cassidy find the truth? Or will her past finally drown her?

Storm Surge

A storm is brewing hundreds of miles away, but its effects are devastating even from afar. Laid-back, loose, and light: that's Cassidy Livingston's new motto. But when a makeshift boat with a bloody cloth inside washes ashore near her oceanfront home, her detective instincts shift into gear . . . again. Seeking clues isn't the only thing on her mind—romance is heating up with next-door neighbor and former Navy SEAL Ty Chambers as well. Her heart wants the love and stability she's longed for her entire life. But her hidden identity only leads to a tidal wave of turbulence. As more answers emerge about the boat, the danger around her rises, creating a treacherous swell that threatens to reveal her past. Can Cassidy mind her own business, or will the storm surge of violence and corruption that has washed ashore on Lantern Beach leave her life in wreckage?

Dangerous Waters

Danger lurks on the horizon, leaving only two choices: find shelter or flee. Cassidy Livingston's new identity has begun to feel as comfortable as her favorite sweater. She's been tucked away on Lantern Beach for weeks, waiting to testify against a deadly gang, and is settling in to a new life she wants to last forever. When she thinks she spots someone malevolent from her past, panic swells inside her. If an enemy has found her, Cassidy won't be the only one who's a target. Everyone she's come to love will also be at risk. Dangerous waters threaten to pull her into an overpowering chasm she may never escape. Can Cassidy survive what lies ahead? Or has the tide fatally turned against her?

Perilous Riptide

Just when the current seems safer, an unseen danger emerges and threatens to destroy everything. When Cassidy Livingston finds a journal hidden deep in the recesses of her ice cream truck, her curiosity kicks into high gear. Islanders suspect that Elsa, the journal's owner, didn't die accidentally. Her final entry indicates their suspicions might be correct and that what Elsa observed on her final night may have led to her demise. Against the advice of Ty Chambers, her former Navy SEAL boyfriend, Cassidy taps into her detective skills and hunts for answers. But her search only leads to a skeletal body and trouble for both of them. As helplessness threatens to drown her, Cassidy is desperate to turn back time. Can Cassidy find what she needs to navigate the perilous situation? Or will the riptide surrounding her threaten everyone and everything Cassidy loves?

Deadly Undertow

The current's fatal pull is powerful, but so is one detective's will to live. When someone from Cassidy Livingston's past shows up on Lantern Beach and warns her of impending peril, opposing currents collide, threatening to drag her under. Running would be easy. But leaving would break her heart. Cassidy must decipher between the truth and lies, between reality and deception. Even more importantly, she must decide whom to trust and whom to fear. Her life depends on it. As danger rises and answers surface, everything Cassidy thought she knew is tested. In order to survive, Cassidy must take drastic measures and end the battle against the ruthless gang DH-7 once and for all. But if her final mission fails, the consequences will be as deadly as the raging undertow.

LANTERN BEACH ROMANTIC SUSPENSE

Tides of Deception

Change has come to Lantern Beach: a new police chief, a new season, and . . . a new romance? Austin Brooks has loved Skye Lavinia from the moment they met, but the walls she keeps around her seem impenetrable. Skye knows Austin is the best thing to ever happen to her. Yet she also knows that if he learns the truth about her past, he'd be a fool not to run. A chance encounter brings secrets bubbling to the surface, and danger soon follows. Are the life-threatening events plaguing them really accidents . . . or is someone trying to send a deadly message? With the tides on Lantern Beach come deception and lies. One question remains—who will be swept away as the water shifts? And will it bring the end for Austin and Skye, or merely the beginning?

Shadow of Intrigue

For her entire life, Lisa Garth has felt like a supporting character in the drama of life. The designation never bothered her—until now. Lantern Beach, where she's settled and runs a popular restaurant, has boarded up for the season. The slower pace leaves her with too much time alone. Braden Dillinger came to Lantern Beach to try to heal. The former Special Forces officer returned from battle with invisible scars and diminished hope. But his recovery is hampered by the fact that an unknown enemy is trying to kill him. From the moment Lisa and Braden meet, danger ignites around them, and both are drawn into a web of intrigue that turns their lives upside down. As shadows creep in, will Lisa and Braden be able to shine a light on the peril around them? Or will the encroaching darkness turn their worst nightmares into reality?

Storm of Doubt

A pastor who's lost faith in God. A romance writer who's lost faith in love. A faceless man with a deadly obsession. Nothing has felt right in Pastor Jack Wilson's world since his wife died two years ago. He hoped coming to Lantern Beach might help soothe the ragged edges of his soul. Instead, he feels more alone than ever. Novelist Juliette Grace came to the island to hide away. Though her professional life has never been better, her personal life has imploded. Her husband left her and a stalker's threats have grown more and more dangerous. When Jack saves Juliette from an attack, he sees the terror in her gaze and knows he must protect her. But when danger strikes again, will Jack be able to keep her safe? Or will the approaching storm prove too strong to withstand?

Winds of Danger

Wes O'Neill is perfectly content to hang with his friends and enjoy island life on Lantern Beach. Something begins to change inside him when Paige Henderson sweeps into his life. But the beautiful newcomer is hiding painful secrets beneath her cheerful facade. Police dispatcher Paige Henderson came to Lantern Beach riddled with guilt and uncertainties after the fallout of a bad relationship. When she meets Wes, she begins to open up to the possibility of love again. But there's something Wes isn't telling her—something that could change everything. As the winds shift, doubts seep into Paige's mind. Can Paige and Wes trust each other, even as the currents work against them? Or is trouble from the past too much to overcome?

Rains of Remorse

A stranger invades her home, leaving Rebecca Jarvis terrified. Above all, she must protect the baby growing inside her. Since her estranged husband died suspiciously six months earlier, Rebecca has been determined to depend on no one but herself. Her chivalrous new neighbor appears to be an answer to prayer. But who is Levi Stoneman really? Rebecca wants to believe he can help her, but she can't ignore her instincts. As danger closes in, both Rebecca and Levi must figure out whom they can trust. With Rebecca's baby coming soon, there's no time to waste. Can the truth prevail . . . or will remorse overpower the best of intentions?

LANTERN BEACH PD

On the Lookout

When Cassidy Chambers accepted the job as police chief on Lantern Beach, she knew the island had its secrets. But a suspicious death with potentially far-reaching implications will test all her skills—and threaten to reveal her true identity. Cassidy enlists the help of her husband, former Navy SEAL Ty Chambers. As they dig for answers, both uncover parts of their pasts that are best left buried. Not everything is as it seems, and they must figure out if their John Doe is connected to the secretive group that has moved onto the island. As facts materialize, danger on the island grows. Can Cassidy and Ty discover the truth about the shadowy crimes in their cozy community? Or has darkness permanently invaded their beloved Lantern Beach?

Attempt to Locate

A fun girls' night out turns into a nightmare when armed robbers barge into the store where Cassidy and her friends are shopping. As the situation escalates and the men escape, a massive manhunt launches on Lantern Beach to apprehend the dangerous trio. In the midst of the chaos, a potential foe asks for Cassidy's help. He needs to find his sister who fled from the secretive Gilead's Cove community on the island. But the more Cassidy learns about the seemingly untouchable group, the more her unease grows. The pressure to solve both cases continues to mount. But as the gravity of the situation rises, so does the danger. Cassidy is determined to protect the island and break up the cult ... but doing so might cost her everything.

First Degree Murder

Police Chief Cassidy Chambers longs for a break from the recent crimes plaguing Lantern Beach. She simply wants to enjoy her friends' upcoming wedding, to prepare for the busy tourist season about to slam the island, and to gather all the dirt she can on the suspicious community that's invaded the town. But trouble explodes on the island, sending residents—including Cassidy—into a squall of uneasiness. Cassidy may have more than one enemy plotting her demise, and the collateral damage seems unthinkable. As the temperature rises, so does the pressure to find answers.

Someone is determined that Lantern Beach would be better off without their new police chief. And for Cassidy, one wrong move could mean certain death.

Dead on Arrival

With a highly charged local election consuming the community, Police Chief Cassidy Chambers braces herself for a challenging day of breaking up petty conflicts and tamping down high emotions. But when widespread food poisoning spreads among potential voters across the island, Cassidy smells something rotten in the air. As Cassidy examines every possibility to uncover what's going on, local enigma Anthony Gilead again comes on her radar. The man is running for mayor and his cult-like following is growing at an alarming rate. Cassidy feels certain he has a spy embedded in her inner circle. The problem is that her pool of suspects gets deeper every day. Can Cassidy get to the bottom of what's eating away at her peaceful island home? Will voters turn out despite the outbreak of illness plaguing their tranquil town? And the even bigger question: Has darkness come to stay on Lantern Beach?

Plan of Action

A missing Navy SEAL. Danger at the boiling point. The ultimate showdown. When Police Chief Cassidy Chambers' husband, Ty, disappears, her world is turned upside down. His truck is discovered with blood inside, crashed in a ditch on Lantern Beach, but he's nowhere to be found. As they launch a manhunt to find him, Cassidy discovers that someone on the island has a deadly obsession with Ty. Meanwhile, Gilead's Cove seems to be imploding. As danger heightens, federal law enforcement officials are called in. The cult's growing threat could lead to the pinnacle standoff of good versus evil. A clear plan of action is needed or the results will be devastating. Will Cassidy find Ty in time, or will she face a gut-wrenching loss? Will Anthony Gilead finally be unmasked for who he really is and be brought to justice? Hundreds of innocent lives are at stake . . . and not everyone will come out alive.

YOU MIGHT ALSO ENJOY ...

THE SQUEAKY CLEAN MYSTERY SERIES

On her way to completing a degree in forensic science, Gabby St. Claire drops out of school and starts her own crime-scene cleaning business. When a routine cleaning job uncovers a murder weapon the police overlooked, she realizes that the wrong person is in jail. She also realizes that crime scene cleaning might be the perfect career for utilizing her investigative skills.

#1 Hazardous Duty
#2 Suspicious Minds
#2.5 It Came Upon a Midnight Crime (novella)
#3 Organized Grime
#4 Dirty Deeds
#5 The Scum of All Fears
#6 To Love, Honor and Perish

#7 Mucky Streak
#8 Foul Play
#9 Broom & Gloom
#10 Dust and Obey
#11 Thrill Squeaker
#11.5 Swept Away (novella)
#12 Cunning Attractions
#13 Cold Case: Clean Getaway
#14 Cold Case: Clean Sweep
#15 Cold Case: Clean Break
While You Were Sweeping, A Riley Thomas Spinoff

THE WORST DETECTIVE EVER:

I'm not really a private detective. I just play one on TV.

Joey Darling, better known to the world as Raven Remington, detective extraordinaire, is trying to separate herself from her invincible alter ego. She played the spunky character for five years on the hit TV show *Relentless*, which catapulted her to fame and into the role of Hollywood's sweetheart. When her marriage falls apart, her finances dwindle to nothing, and her father disappears, Joey finds herself on the Outer Banks of North Carolina, trying to piece together her life away from the limelight. But as people continually mistake her for the character she played on TV, she's tasked with solving real life crimes . . . even though she's terrible at it.

#1 Ready to Fumble
#2 Reign of Error
#3 Safety in Blunders
#4 Join the Flub
#5 Blooper Freak
#6 Flaw Abiding Citizen
#7 Gaffe Out Loud
#8 Joke and Dagger
#9 Wreck the Halls
#10 Glitch and Famous (coming soon)

ABOUT THE AUTHOR

USA Today has called Christy Barritt's books "scary, funny, passionate, and quirky."

Christy writes both mystery and romantic suspense novels that are clean with underlying messages of faith. Her books have won the Daphne du Maurier Award for Excellence in Suspense and Mystery, have been twice nominated for the Romantic Times Reviewers' Choice Award, and have finaled for both a Carol Award and Foreword Magazine's Book of the Year.

She is married to her Prince Charming, a man who thinks she's hilarious—but only when she's not trying to be. Christy is a self-proclaimed klutz, an avid music lover who's known for spontaneously bursting into song, and a road trip aficionado.

When she's not working or spending time with her family, she enjoys singing, playing the guitar, and exploring small, unsuspecting towns where people have no idea how accident-prone she is.

Find Christy online at:
   www.christybarritt.com
   www.facebook.com/christybarritt
   www.twitter.com/cbarritt

Sign up for Christy's newsletter to get information on all of her latest releases here: www.christybarritt.com/newsletter-sign-up/

If you enjoyed this book, please consider leaving a review.

Made in the USA
Monee, IL
29 June 2021